SEEING RED

THE IMPERIUM COAST SERIES
BOOK 2

ALACIA HALE

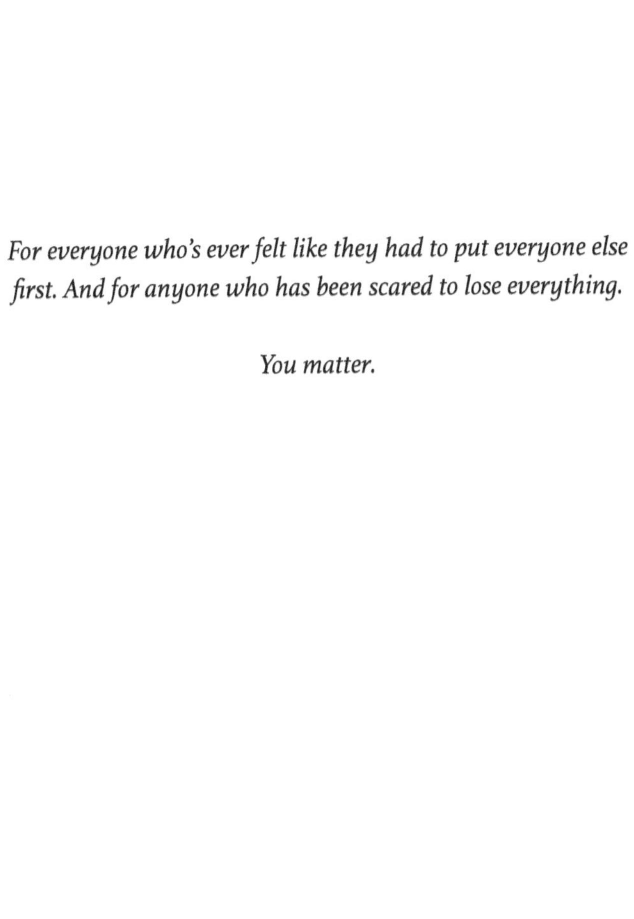

For everyone who's ever felt like they had to put everyone else first. And for anyone who has been scared to lose everything.

You matter.

TROPES & CONTENT WARNINGS

Tropes

Multi-POV, brother's best friend, university romance, situationship, secret friends with benefits, gym buddies, can't stay away

Content Warnings

This book deals with themes that may be distressing to some readers including parental divorce and neglect, blackmail, and underage drinking.

Seeing Red also contains open door sex scenes between two characters and include mentions of masturbation, dominance, and light age play. The main female character is also a freshman in college.

If any of these elements are distressing to you, *please protect your mental health.*

1

Fifteen

This big, poofy dress fucking chafes. The powder blue horror-show itches like hell and the dark navy straps cut into my shoulders.

I've been poked and prodded since eight this morning when Mom floated into my room with what seemed like thirty yards of gauzy material over her arm and three women I never met before in my life. I spawned a smile when she held up the dress to see my reaction before handing it off to one of the newcomers and promptly leaving me to be bathed and buffed by strangers.

Now, alone for the first time in hours, I walk over to my floor length mirror and see myself for the first time. The pile of mosquito netting falls over my body creating a thick barrier between me and anything trying to get closer than a foot to my body. A giant piece of cobalt satin wraps around my waist forming a huge bow on the center of my back and some sort of human shape out of the pile of material ensconcing me.

My hair has been straightened and forced back into a tight bun. Two giant teardrop pearls hang from my earlobes. My eyes look bigger with thick lashes drenched in mascara and light blue eyeshadow over my lids. My lips shine, glossy and pink, in the overhead lighting and my shoulders sparkle with the shimmery mist one of the women sprayed me in hours ago.

I don't recognize a single part of my reflection.

Gripping fistfuls of the scratchy material at my hips, I exhale slowly. Light pink would have been better than this, though a deep red would have been preferred. And none of this gauzy floaty crap.

Plus, I feel naked without a scrunchie on my wrist to occupy my hands.

I glance over at the strappy shoes. They fortunately have short chunky heels, but that seems to be their only redeeming quality. I wonder how much longer I can get away with not putting them on.

Someone knocks at my bedroom door.

"Come in," I shout over my shoulder.

The door opens to reveal my mom, adorned in an elegant floor length gown that swirls around her feet as she steps into the doorway. Her hair sits in a perfectly circular bun atop her head, the strands a similar dark brown to mine, but peppered with silvery grays. Ramsey stands behind her in the hall, his usual dark curls slicked back and a clean-cut tux in place. He smirks over Mom's shoulder when his eyes hit me.

Mom's face, however, lights up and she claps her hands together, bringing them to her mouth. I plaster on another grin when tears gather in her eyes, and she gushes. "You look beautiful, baby." She leaves the doorway, coming up to inspect me from head to toe. Ramsey leans against the doorframe and I narrow my eyes at the mirth in my brother's face.

Harley Sanders appears in the hall behind Ramsey, and I fight the sudden urge to fidget. My eyes glance over him, noticing the way his tux fits his athletic frame. He adjusts his cufflinks, teeth chewing on the inside of his cheek as he concentrates. His usually free-falling hair is tied back at the nape of his neck, but a few inky black pieces have escaped to frame his face. Shuffling his shoulders, he looks up, pausing to inspect me before a familiar mocking smirk tips the corner of his mouth.

I glare at him, ignoring how my stomach flips at his appearance.

Mom ends her tour around my dress and stops to stand before me. "What do you think?"

I grab her white gloved hands and beam. "I love it," I say as cheerily as I can and hear Ramsey snort.

He crosses his arms over his chest. "She looks like a cloud, Mom."

Our mother releases one of my hands and turns toward my brother and his best friend. "Ramsey Adams, do not make fun of your sister on her birthday."

Harley now leans against the opposite side of the door from Ramsey. He moves his hands to his pockets and his grey eyes inspect the carpet.

Ramsey shrugs. "Fine, I'll wait until tomorrow."

Mom scoffs at him with a scowl, and he chuckles. Harley's face remains passive, but his eyes suddenly come up to meet mine and I freeze in place.

"Maybe it is a bit much," Mom says, peering back over me, and I tear my gaze from Harley's to shake my head.

"No, it's great, Mom!" I insist.

Her face lifts, and my anxiety momentarily ceases.

It comes back in full force when she says, "Alrighty, get your shoes on and I'll let the emcee know you're going to be down in a few minutes." She squeezes my hand, and I grit my teeth back into a smile before she lets go and rushes out of the room.

My face falls once she disappears, and Ramsey snickers while I glare at the shoes. I grab them and sit on my bed unsure how to get them on around this skirt.

"Should have told her you hate this," Ramsey says, walking into my room and kneeling in front of me. He grabs the shoe from my hand and my corresponding ankle.

"She gets so excited every year." I flop back on the bed as he fastens the buckle and moves on to the other shoe.

"It's your birthday party. You should get some say in it," Harley says from the doorway. My eyes flit over to him. He stares me down and Ramsey stands up. My brother holds out his hands and I break eye contact with Harley, leaning forward. Ramsey pulls me up and waits while I teeter a bit before settling on the heels.

"He's not wrong." Ramsey cocks his brow and my eyes dip down to the floor.

We have this nonargument every year, ever since Ramsey spoke up about no longer wanting Mom's special brand of birthday fanfare the week before he turned thirteen. I watched a little bit of the light dim in Mom's eyes that day, so I've allowed the grandiose charade to continue every September without complaint. And every year, Ramsey and Harley push me to say something about how much I hate them. But I always wave them off, letting Mom plan another over the top ball and invite a million people I don't know into our house yet again.

I just want to get the next few hours over with.

"It's one day," I say to the ground then pan my eyes back up to Ramsey. "I'm not going to ruin her fun."

Ramsey rolls his eyes, but I see the understanding there too. He knows why I let Mom do this.

Ramsey drops my hands and extends his arm out to me. I take it, and we turn to face Harley. He shakes his head and stands up.

"Today is supposed to be about you having fun."

I feel my face flame as we walk up to him, hoping the makeup hides my reaction. My neck cranes once we stand before my brother's best friend, who continues to block our path. He tilts his head down to meet my eyes, and I grip Ramsey a bit tighter for a moment.

"Last chance to run, Mira," he whispers down to me.

I mechanically shake my head and my throat dries up.

Humming, he murmurs, "Suit yourself." Nodding to my brother and with a quick, "I'll see you down there," he walks away.

Ramsey covers my hand with his and I realize I've been digging my nails into his bicep. I relinquish my grip. "S-sorry."

"Mira," he says, and I hone in. We start to walk down the hallway and toward the boisterous noise emanating from beneath us. "You're going to be okay. I won't let you fall."

"I know." I give him a genuine smile and we reach the top of the stairs. The music suddenly stops, and the din of chatter peters out. People turn to stare up at us with dazzled expressions.

We take our first step down and a loud voice calls out over the speakers, "Ladies and gentlemen, please welcome the guest of honor and birthday girl, Amiria Nicole Adams!"

Applause roars around us and I resume my death grip

on Ramsey's arm. Cameras flash at the bottom of the stairs. We artfully smile and continue to descend leisurely, though each step feels like it sinks iron spikes a little further into my stomach. Ramsey's thumb rubs over my knuckles when we near the bottom and pause with three steps to go so the photographers can take the photos Mom wants. The applause wears down and I see Mom beaming beside my father's colleagues while people shout *happy birthday* all around us.

Kids from school join the fray when Ramsey pulls me down the rest of the stairs and into the crowd. I repeat *thank you* what feels like a thousand times while he walks me around the room in the customary tour before leading me to the giant checkerboard dance floor set up beneath the ever-looming chandelier of our grand foyer. Couples take their places around us, and the emcee starts the waltz Mom picked out for the first dance of the night. I glance over Ramsey's shoulder while we spin around the floor, noting familiar faces and who in the room to avoid.

My eyes find Harley leaning back against a wall, tucked into the shadow under the upstairs balcony, with his hands in his pockets. The rest of Ramsey's friends stand around him. Royal Reznikov appears extremely relaxed in his usual suit directly on Harley's left. Tanner Hill stands off to the right, his signature pale white hair falling past his shoulders which seem constrained in the tight tuxedo jacket stretched across them. He glares down at Royal's cousin, Smith Reznikov, who stands in front of the group and gestures wildly, seemingly arguing with Tanner as per usual. Tanner barely moves, watching Smith sip from a flask and rolling his eyes while his erratic friend pulls a blonde into his side. More girls, in much nicer dresses than mine, flit around the group, each hoping to for a chance to be noticed by the infamous former Emerald Grove Ravens.

Harley's eyes stay on Ramsey and me though, watching us dance. When our eyes meet, he smirks, knowing how much I'm fighting the urge to squirm in the spotlight. I tamp down the reflex to stick my tongue out at him and he snorts.

We spin and I lose sight of him and my footing. Ramsey cringes when I step on his foot beneath the miles of blue mesh surrounding us.

"Sorry," I mumble, and he laughs, getting me back on the next step. I hold back a wince and hiss, "Really?!"

He laughs more and the dance stops a moment later, each of us stepping back to applaud with the rest of the crowd. More people say happy birthday to me when we exit the dance floor, only obligated to partake in the first dance. Food and drinks line several tables around the room, and I dash to the one with the mini grilled cheeses and tomato soup fountain. It is the only thing in this room I had any real input on when going over the party details.

I grab a porcelain cup and start filling it from the fountain. Ramsey shakes his head next to me.

"Awful dress."

I jolt at the familiar voice and Ramsey lurches forward to keep the cup of soup upright in my hand. I let him take it and whirl around to find Bentley Marshall standing before me. I squeal and jump into his open arms.

"When did you get back?" I yell and engulf my best friend.

He chuckles in my ear, arms wrapping around me. Gravity kicks in, pulling the weight of my dress back to Earth, but Bentley just leans down, extending our hug. "Last night. Figured I'd surprise you." He squeezes me before releasing.

I slap his arm, pulling a dramatic pout when we pull apart. "You could have told me you'd be here tonight! It would have helped my nerves." My pout melts into a huge grin as I stare at my best friend in person for the first time in two months.

He's tanner than I last saw him, his already sun kissed skin more bronze than honey hued. His bright hazel eyes shine and he grins back at me. I take a breath of relief and I realize I won't have to cling to my big brother and his friends all night.

"As if I'd miss your birthday party, Mir," Bentley says with an over-the-top eye roll. "Not even the beaches in Venice could keep me away."

"I'm leaving her in your hands, Marshall," Ramsey says, putting my cup of soup down on the table beside us. "If she gets drunk again, I'm holding you responsible." He wags his finger at Bentley who rolls his eyes at my brother. Ramsey may have caught us sneaking some champagne last year and he has yet to let me hear the end of it.

"Aye, aye, Adams." Bentley stands up straighter and gives Ramsey a fake salute. My brother pinches the bridge of his nose, walking away from us.

I start to pile a plate with mini grilled cheeses and grab my cooled cup of soup. We head over to one of the small standing height tables around the room and Bentley starts telling me about the fiasco his parents endured at the airport yesterday when they almost got denied entry to the airline's first-class lounge. I laugh, picturing his mom's horror and his father's shock at being denied anything. But my eyes watch the extravagant couples dance and I picture myself twirling with a certain black-haired giant currently fist bumping my brother against the opposite wall.

I dig into my sandwiches, contenting myself to just enjoy this one thing tonight.

Mom's laugh echoes through the room, breaking me from my daydream. I find her nearby, head thrown back, hand over her stomach as she grips her friend's arm. They laugh along with her. My lips turn up while I watch her straighten and wipe a tear from her eye, continuing a conversation with a small group. I search around the room for my father but see no sign of him. I'm sure if I wander up to his office, I'll find him either alone or with several other men, all trying to make deals over scotch and cigars.

I wonder if Mom ever daydreams about dancing with Dad, like they used to.

The party is in full swing, and Bentley and I have hidden in the backyard. A new girl, Autumn, came tearing outside, running full tilt toward the tree line at the edge of our property. When we finally caught up to her, it took a few minutes to calm her down before we realized my brother of all people made her flee.

Starting to head back toward the party again, I comment, "Should be easy enough to avoid Ramsey since he's just home for the weekend. He's at university this year." Autumn's head perks up, so I add. "And he took his wolf pack with him." Bentley snickers and Autumn snorts.

I grin before movement in my peripheral pulls my attention to the dark righthand corner. Harley leans against the ledge, his arms folded over his chest, unamused.

Bentley starts telling Autumn about the sushi station by the kitchen, so I quietly throw out, "I'll be right there, guys." They open the door to rejoin the party with quick nods to me. Bentley smirks after noticing Harley and then they are gone, the door muffling the noise of the party.

I walk toward Harley, and he tosses out, "Wolf pack?"

Shaking my head, I bite back my smile and rest my hands on the ledge before I lean against it beside him. "Would you prefer murder of ravens?"

Harley's eyes fly skyward. He continues to face the opposite direction. A moment passes where we just stand beside each other comfortably.

Harley has to ruin it. "Hiding from the crowd or running away and got stopped by Marshall?"

"I wasn't running away."

"Hiding then." He smirks. "Probably a better plan. Ramsey would be pissed if you ran off without him."

I almost ask him how he would feel about it but the knots in my stomach twist too much. "I was looking for Autumn after she ran out here. Didn't want her to get lost or end up wandering out to your yard." The Sander's property line touches ours somewhere in the middle of the outcropping of trees separating our two lawns.

Harley turns toward me and lifts a challenging brow. "You shouldn't meddle in your brother's shit."

I sag against the stone wall. "Not like he keep his nose out of mine."

Harley snorts. "You got something going on that Ramsey would be interested in?"

I slide my eyes over to his face. "Not anything I'd share with you, guard dog number two."

His jaw ticks, before he smiles without glee. "Just remember, he always figures out whatever it is you try to hide."

I roll my eyes and ignore the heat blazing my cheeks.

"Not all the way from college," I say smugly. He shakes his head. "How are you liking it?"

"College?" he asks, and I nod. He shrugs and glances over at the party through the glass doors. I follow his line of sight, seeing the mountain of shiny gifts on a table in the corner. A giant obviously easel-shaped gift stands off to the side and I grin, knowing Bentley will drag me over to see it when I go back inside.

"Your mom was looking for you. Something about it almost being time for cake." He pushes off the wall. "Should probably get back."

I turn to follow him, but he stops, and I end up stood before him. I stare up at his face and he tilts his head down.

"Happy birthday, Meerkat."

My heart rate spikes at the familiar nickname, and I reach out to grab his arm. I freeze at the contact, and he waits. Opening my mouth, I blurt out, "What did you get me?"

Harley furrows his brow. "What?"

"For my birthday. What did you get me?" I let go of his arm, suddenly very aware that we are touching.

Harley pauses a moment before saying, "My mom probably put your gift on the table when she got here."

I nod. "Right." My chin tips down.

"I think it was something off that registry your mom set up."

"Oh great." I peek back at the trees behind the house again. That running away plan sounds good right now. I shake my head, eyes back on Harley. "Probably some fucking curling wand or earring set then."

He grins when I swear, but then seems to frown when the rest of my words filtered in. "What do you want?"

My forehead creases and I shake my head. "What do you mean?"

Harley leans a little closer to me. "For your birthday. What do you want?" He stares at me, waiting.

I think hard about what I want. Harley has never given me a birthday gift without his parents' or Ramsey's name attached. I know I could ask for almost anything and he would try to get it for me. He's always been just as passionate as Ramsey when it comes to reminding me that my birthday should be about me.

An idea pops into my head and without another thought, I just act. In a move I've done a thousand times this summer alone, I hoist myself up onto the stone ledge behind me, knowing Harley will step closer to put his hand on my waist and make sure I don't fall. I throw an arm around his neck when he does and pull his head toward mine, managing to mumble, "I want this," just before I crash my lips to his and heat explodes across my skin.

I thought my face flamed when I saw him before, but that heat has nothing on the blaze that seems to ignite my lips where they touch his. His grip on my waist tightens.

Then he is gone.

I open my eyes to see him stumble back from me, shock painting his face.

"Are you drunk again?" he asks, anger momentarily clouding his eyes.

"No," I squeak, frozen to the ledge. My body locks up as if one move and I'll actually have to acknowledge the mortifying reality I've created for myself.

Harley swears and spins toward the doors, taking two steps, before whipping back around to face me. His eyes burn into me, and I suppress a shiver down my spine when I see actual hatred in his eyes for a second. "You shouldn't have done that," he spits out before fleeing back into the party.

I stare at the door long after it closes. I don't realize for a good few minutes that my body is shaking, and I broke more than one nail digging them into the stone beneath me. With a shuddering breath, I finally let go of the tension in my body and rejection washes over me in a venomous wave.

I somehow managed to make this the worst birthday yet.

2

Three Years Later

Moving day. It's finally here.

When Ramsey left for Imperium Coast University, Mom and I helped move him into his dorm. I remember staring up at West Tower dorms and being floored by how much I wanted to be moving too. Seeing the freedom Ramsey and Harley were about to experience, envy expanded in my chest. And that little seed of envy made itself known every time Ramsey came home and told me about his time at college.

The only thing that assuaged it was daydreaming about this day, when I would finally get to move into my own dorm with my best friends and start a whole new adventure together.

Standing in the doorway of my soon-to-be-freedom, I breathe, feeling that envy finally loosen and float away.

"Move," Ramsey blurts, his back bumping into me.

I quickly jump to the side, clutching a box to my chest so

that he can plow through the suite toward my new bedroom, Tanner in tow. The two carry a large cardboard box containing my new unassembled dresser that finally arrived two days ago. Disappearing, the duo leaves me behind in the common room, but Royal, Smith, and my mom follow closely, each carrying different boxes and bags. Bentley brings up the rear, carrying nothing with a grin on his face.

I roll my eyes at him as he walks up. "Shouldn't you be moving into your own room?"

"Mommy and Daddy dearest got movers to handle setting things up. I'm not to go bother them until after lunch." My brows arch, and he shrugs. "Not all of us have a harem of men to help move all our stuff in for free."

"Not for free," Smith says, coming out empty handed and throwing his arm over my shoulders. "Mini-Adams owes us big for this, right, *dorogaya*?" He waggles his eyebrows at me with a smirk. So, I shove the box in my arms into his stomach.

He grunts and I smile sweetly up at him. "Better not let Ramsey hear you hitting on me." I drop my arms from the box and Smith pulls his arm from my shoulders to grab it before it falls.

Bentley chuckles and Ramsey, Tanner, and Royal emerge from my room.

"Already heard, and your death has been noted in my planner, Reznikov." Ramsey grabs the collar of his shirt as they pass and starts dragging him out to get more stuff from the truck downstairs.

"At least let me live through the opening weekend of parties," Smith begs and tosses the box back at me, forcing me to launch forward and grab it before it can hit the floor. I groan and Bentley takes the box, putting it on the couch nearby. We stand in the dorm, finally getting a chance to hunt around.

Room 608 is really a suite of rooms, the front door opening to a large but cozy common room. Green couches center around a gold painted metal coffee table atop a plush black rug that looks soft enough to sleep on. A short, dark wood entertainment center sits against the wall the couches face with a decent sized TV on top of it.

Beside the front door, an archway set into the perpendicular wall shows a small white and black themed kitchen with stainless steel appliances. The wall opposite that one has an ajar door, revealing a bathroom with two sinks and a glass walled shower. And across from us has my open bedroom door and an identical closed door beside it, waiting for my new roommate to show up.

A smile grows on my face. "I love this place."

My mom pops her head around the corner. "You better, considering how much your father and I are paying for it." She smiles before disappearing into my bedroom again.

I shake my head.

Bentley nods. "I will never understand why your brother moved out after his freshman year."

"You haven't seen Royal and Smith's mansion," I mutter. "Have you seen Autumn yet?" I had a full breakfast at home with my family, Bentley, and his grandfather before Ramsey and Mom drove us down. But Autumn would have wanted to get here and away from her family as soon as possible.

"Nah, she's probably still organizing her closet by color." Bentley picks up the box off the couch and nods toward my room. "I think she said she's 317 so we can go see her after you're done."

I take the box from him. "She's 315," I say, stopping in the doorway of my room.

My bedspread lays across a full-sized bed centered in front of a large window. Mom stands to one side, fluffing a pillow. She watches as I walk in and put the box down on the dark wood desk matching the headboard on the bed. A side table sits to the left of the bed and the wall opposite the desk houses a floor to ceiling closet with open accordion doors. Beyond the window sits the whole of campus. West Tower sits on the edge of Ring Road which encloses the entire school grounds, fenced in completely with only four wrought iron gates allowing people in and out. From this high up, I can see the tall cathedral spires of the library in the center of all the brick academic buildings.

"Looks small from up here." Bentley nudges my shoulder, and I smirk at him.

"It'll look bigger when you're trying to find the right building tomorrow," I tease.

"Harley can probably give you a tour of the poli-sci building. They share with the English department."

I whirl around at the sound of Royal's voice and Harley's name. Just mentioning him still makes my pulse race and I chastise myself every time for the reaction.

The boys return with the rest of my stuff, dropping it in random areas around the room.

"Thought he was working?" Bentley says and leans against the wall, putting his hand on my shoulder to squeeze it quickly. I broke down after my fifteenth birthday party and Bentley stayed the night, listening to my terrible rejected kiss story and hugging me till the tears dried.

"He is, but he's out at three." Ramsey plops down on the floor and flicks open a switchblade. He starts cutting the tape off the box my dresser came in.

"Maybe he can show you where the chemistry buildings are too," Mom says. She opens a bag and starts hanging up clothes in my closet. I snap the elastic of the scarlet satin scrunchie adorning my wrist.

Smith drops into my desk chair and leans back, propping his feet up on the desk. "Sanders barely knew where his own classes were let alone anyone else's."

We all turn to him. Royal stands nearby with his arms crossed.

Smith tips his head back and closes his eyes. "You'd be better off getting a tour from literally anyone else."

Tanner snorts from the floor, having sat down opposite Ramsey to help him construct the dresser. "He's not wrong."

"I'm sure Harley knows where his classes were," Mom says, smoothing the shoulder of the shirt she just hung up. She looks over at Bentley while she grabs the next garment from the duffel bag. "And he got through his first semester before he dropped out, so he should know where all the classes you're taking are, Bentley."

I feel another squeeze on my shoulder, having stayed stock still through the entire exchange. "He probably does know his way around that part of campus, Mrs. Adams," Bentley says. "I'll text him later to see."

Mom beams before turning back to the closet.

Bentley has barely acknowledged Harley since my fifteenth, so that text is never getting sent.

"This thing didn't come with an allen wrench," Ramsey exclaims, throwing the directions on the pile of parts he and Tanner just unpacked. Tanner starts picking up all the Styrofoam and paper and packing it back into the box. Ramsey addresses me. "I have a few back at the house. I can come by later to set this up."

I nod, eyeing the pile of wood that will probably live on my floor for a month before Ramsey remembers to come back for it. I might need to find the tool somewhere in town so I can at least attempt putting it together myself at some point.

"Knock, knock," a new voice makes everyone's head turn toward the door.

A tall, brown-haired girl stands in my doorway, beaming at us with a clipboard in her hands. Her gaze zeroes in on me, ignoring all the men strewn about, and I startle. Her eyes are two different colors.

"Amiria?"

"Mira," I say, stepping around my brother on the floor. Tanner continues to pack away the trash, the other Ravens seeming to already know the newcomer. Smith opens his eyes at her arrival, smirking when he takes her in.

She hugs me once I clear Ramsey, and I awkwardly hug her back. "I'm Gwen, your RA. Welcome to the Coast!" she gushes, leaning back. Up close, her eyes are beautiful, the left a rich brown with small patches of icy blue that matches most of her right, though that pupil has a ring of deep brown around the edge and cones of gold running throughout. She giggles and I realize I've just been staring at her like a freak.

"Sorry," I say, shaking my head a little. "I mean, thank you." I step back, breaking the hug and feeling my nerves settle a bit with some distance.

"The eyes, right?" Gwen says, leaning her clipboard against her hip. "Most people stare a little when they first see them." She smiles kindly and I return it.

"Hi, I'm April Adams, Mira's mom." My mother steps forward and shakes Gwen's hand. Gwen's smile seems to grow in wattage as she returns the handshake.

"Hi, Ms. Adams. I'm sure you have questions."

"Mom," Ramsey says, a warning in his tone. "You already

interrogated the RA when I moved here. You don't need to do that again with Gwenivere."

Gwen's face pinches at her full name, but her lips stay firmly upturned. "It's okay, Ramsey. She can ask me anything." Mom nods her head at Gwen before pulling her over the pile of dresser pieces to the closet.

"Think my RA is that hot?" Bentley whispers in my ear. I slap his chest. He chuckles.

Tanner stands with the box of trash and Ramsey stands up too, putting his hands in his pockets. Tanner comes over and wraps me into a quick one-armed side hug. "I'll probably see you around campus before your party next weekend but have a good first week, Mini-Adams."

"Thanks, Tan. Good luck in your scrimmage tomorrow. Does knowing the goalie get me free tickets to any of the Arctic Fox home games?"

Tanner just laughs, shaking his head. He starts to walk out with the trash and throws a *bye* to Mom. Gwen glances over at him too, but he resolutely avoids her, eyes passing over her as he leaves.

Smith bounds from the chair to my side. He grasps my shoulders and kisses both my cheeks, then sends a wink to my brother over my shoulder. "We can't make your party next weekend. Family thing. But I will definitely get you a drink at your actual party next Wednesday."

Ramsey pries his hands from my shoulders, stepping in front of me. "I don't think so," he says, walking him to the door with an arm around his neck that looks flexed more than it needs to be.

Royal chuckles at the two of them. "Have a good week, little Adams. Sorry we're missing your big party."

I shake my head and smile at him. He grabs my hand and gives it a squeeze before following the others out.

"Probably a good thing the Russians won't be there this year," Bentley says, falling to lie on a cleared section of my bed. He puts his hands behind his head "We wouldn't want a repeat of last year's vodka fiasco." Smith thought it would be funny to spike the drink fountain at my seventeenth last year. Only the fountain was made of champagne and meant for the over twenty-one crowd anyway so all he really did was piss off a bunch of my parent's friends.

I push Bentley's feet off my bed with a glare at his shoes and he sits up before he can fall completely off the bed.

Ramsey walks back in, leaning against the wall next to the door and eyeing Gwen for a minute before glancing at me.

"You could always call it off," he muses.

"What are you calling off?" Mom asks, her hand on Gwen's back. They step back over the dresser pieces.

"Nothing, Mom," I reply after shooting Ramsey a quick glare. He tried at least once every week this summer to convince me to call off my birthday party, but he'd usually have given up by now in previous years.

He shrugs and crosses his arms over his chest.

"Well, here are your keys," Gwen says, handing me a set of two keys with a little copper piece adorned with 608A on the keyring. "One's for the suite and one's for your room. I'm suite 601, just down the hall. Anything you need, any problem you have, feel free to come and see me. I have my class schedule up next to my door. You should have gotten my cell number in your orientation packet. If it's an emergency and I'm out, you can text me or go to any of the other floors. The RAs are all in the 01 suites." She smiles at everyone in turn and seems to need to take a breath after saying everything in just a few seconds. "First floor meeting is tonight at seven in the open lounge. Next to my room. By the stairs. Hope you have a good first day and I'll see you tonight!" She waves before heading out, glancing over at the door beside mine. Janette must still not be here because she just rolls her shoulders before crossing the common room and leaving the suite.

"Alright, missy," Mom sidles up to my side and wraps an arm around my waist. "Do you want me to stay and help you put things away or just want me to take you to lunch and head home after?"

Remembering how she broke down, crying about her baby boy leaving the nest when Ramsey moved here, I suppress a shudder.

"Let's do lunch. I can unpack all this later."

Ramsey smirks and Bentley claps his hands together.

"We going to Romero's?"

Mom nods. Bentley has tagged along on plenty of visits to see Ramsey over the years, so he knows my mom's favorite local restaurant.

"Sweet." He follows me and Mom out.

Ramsey pushes off the wall and brings up the rear. We head to the elevator and Ramsey pulls his keys from his pocket. "Just got to stop at the house and drop off Harley's truck. I'll meet you guys there."

My spine snaps straight. "That's Harley's truck?" The elevator starts to descend, and I pretend that causes my stomach to start squirming.

Ramsey pulls his phone out, nodding and responding to a text. Bentley moves closer, his shoulder touching mine.

Mom grins. "That was nice of him, lending his truck since he couldn't be here."

I lean back against the bar on the wall and hum noncommittally.

Harley has barely looked at me in the last three years.

Any time he spoke around me, my family's proximity forced the issue.

But he lent his truck to help me move. The gesture seems sweet, though ultimately benign. Maybe enough time has gone by that we can forget about the kiss. Maybe we can go back to the friendship we had before, now that we live in the same town again. My heart slams in my chest while I walk behind everyone to the parking lot beside West Tower.

"Mira! Bentley!" We turn toward Autumn's voice, finding her walking up with a tiny porcelain looking girl. Mom says she'll go get the car and the three of us turn to watch Autumn and the new girl approach. The girl's straight black bob bows against her chin in the light breeze and some strands stick to the black lipstick adorning her lips. Autumn waves cheerily and the newcomer's bright blue eyes dissect our group. They pop, surrounded in thick kohl liner ending in a sharp point on either side. Her black shirt falls off one shoulder and she wears ripped, jean shorts with fishnet tights and platform combat boots. Even with the extra height, the top of her head probably only comes to my shoulder. Tattoos peek out between the holes of her tights on her thighs, and I admire the work on the left, a wolf snarling with its jaw open.

"Guys, this is my roommate, Aria," Autumn gestures to the girl beside her. Ramsey nods to the newcomer, before walking away and heading to where he parked the truck.

"Don't mind, Ramsey," Autumn says. "He has a permanent stick up his ass."

"Mira," I say with a smile and point at Bentley.

He gives a short wave. "Bentley. You'll probably be seeing a lot of us."

Aria laughs. "Fine by me." She shrugs. "I'm used to a chaotic house, so I don't mind extra company."

"You guys heading to lunch?" Autumn asks. Mom pulls up by the curb nearby.

We nod. "April's taking us to Romero's," Bentley exclaims.

"It's an Italian place in town that he loves," I say to Aria when her forehead scrunches. "There's room in the car if you guys want to come?"

"You want to?" Autumn asks Aria and the smaller girl nods, smiling.

"Will your mom mind?"

I laugh. "Definitely not. She would have to contend with my brother and this one," I say, jerking my thumb toward Bentley. "I'm sure she'll love having some more feminine energy around for a bit."

"Hey, April loves me," Bentley argues.

"Okay," Aria nods with a smirk at Bentley's faux outrage.

We turn toward the car and Bentley takes the front seat while Aria and Autumn slide into the back. Ramsey pulls up behind us in the truck and honks the horn while I still stand on the curb. My head whips over and Ramsey gestures for me to come over. I shut the door behind Autumn and walk over to the truck, leaning against the passenger side as he rolls the window down.

"Why is Autumn getting in the car?" He white knuckles the steering wheel.

"Because she's coming to lunch with us." I roll my shoulders, knowing my brother doesn't like my best friend but ignoring it whenever one of them insists on making it obvious.

He rolls his eyes. "You couldn't make some excuse about a last meal with Mom or something?"

"And take Bentley along but not her? She'll sit far away

from you, or you can just skip the meal or something. I'm sure Mom won't mind."

Ramsey groans thinking it over. He knows Mom will be upset if he skips this lunch right now. I glance back just as Mom pulls away from the curb. Walking away from the truck and waving, I hang my head. she left without me.

"Fuck." I head back over to Ramsey.

"Guess I can't skip now. She probably thought you decided to ride with me." He unlocks the door. I pull it open and climb in.

"Bentley probably insisted they get there right away, or we might not get a table." I roll my eyes, picturing him convincing Mom.

I pull on my seatbelt and Ramsey pulls off the curb. As it clicks into place so does the fact that I currently sit in Harley's truck. I helped pack it with my stuff last night, but at the time I had no idea it was Harley's. Now it feels like stepping too far into his life, like I am doing something wrong by sitting in the cab without him knowing. I squirm a bit, seeing if anything of his lies around. Nothing litters the floor or fills the cupholders between Ramsey and I, but a Yankee Candle car scent hangs from the rearview mirror. I watch it fly around with the movements of the car. The side that shows the scent name faces away from me, but the deep red wax inside faintly smells like cranberries.

Ramsey drives five minutes off campus to the huge two-story house he and the Ravens have lived in since Harley dropped out in their freshman year. I spend the entire ride fiddling with the scarlet silk scrunchie wrapped around my wrist. Bees seem to be nesting in my gut and have decided to make themselves known.

We pull up to the black Gothic mansion and I distractedly wonder if Royal or Smith own the place or if their family bought it for them. We always just call it the Ravens' mansion, the semantics of ownership not really of concern.

Unbuckling my seatbelt when the engine goes quiet, I start to get out when I hear Ramsey call out after leaving the truck.

"What are you doing back this early? Thought you were working till three?"

"Got off early," Harley replies, and my heart speeds up. I scramble out of the cab and slam the door harder than intended.

Harley's head twists in my direction, our eyes meeting over the bed of the truck. For a second, I hold onto the idea that him lending the truck means we could get back on good terms. But then his grey eyes seem to freeze over, and his lips turn down before he slides his gaze back to my brother.

"Gotta go shower," he says, starting to head inside.

My stomach plummets, the bees all freezing to death.

I walk around the front of the truck, still hanging back as Ramsey calls out, "We're getting Romero's for lunch. Want me to bring anything back?"

Harley turns to walk backwards, his eyes sliding right past me to Ramsey. "Garlic bread and chicken parm?"

Ramsey nods and tosses Harley his keys. He catches them easily before turning back around and disappearing inside. I stare at the door after it closes before following Ramsey.

3

Harley

miria Adams plagues me. She has for the last three years. Ever since that stupid kiss. And seeing her in my driveway, knowing she's attending the Coast, burns.

So, I head inside.

Royal glances up from the couch when I walk in.

"New guy never showed," I say. "Had nothing to do with no one to show around and nobody to fill my personal training slot, so I left early." He nods, unpausing his game, the volume assaulting me as I start to ascend the stairs.

"You could have come help us move Mira in," Smith says when I pass him on the stairs. He jumps the back of the couch, landing beside Royal and throwing his arms behind his head.

"Doesn't seem like you guys needed the help, since you're back here already." I pause, knowing Smith will probably have another comment and feel slighted if I don't stick around to hear it.

"She didn't bring a lot of stuff," Royal comments instead.

She wouldn't have. She already knows the dorms are

well stocked with furniture and she never really had a lot of things lying around. I doubt her stuff even took up half my truck bed.

"Only took us two trips to bring it all in."

"Probably didn't need your help really then either." I take another step, really needing to wash off the sweat from my shift.

"We're always there for mini-Adams," Smith says, turning his head to meet my eyes. "And I got to kiss her before we left."

My shoulders stiffen and my eyes narrow.

That night Mira kissed me; we had all been sent to go find her so she could cut the cake. Smith just so happened to be passing by the back doors at the opportune moment and witnessed the only moment of my life I could never tell Ramsey about. And he has lorded it over my head ever since.

Smith grins at my glare, before turning back to face the TV. "Just pecks on the cheek, Har. Nothing Ramsey would kill us for."

Royal snorts. I sometimes wonder if Smith shared the details of what he saw with his cousin, but Royal has never let on or teased me the way Smith does.

"I'm sure he doesn't see it that way," I grumble before making it the rest of the way up the stairs and away from my overly confident friend. Ramsey might be the one known for resorting to violence, but I sometimes feel plenty punchy when Smith gets on a roll about things. I make it to my room and do a count down from ten, closing my eyes at five and seeing Mira standing next to my truck, face flushed and eyes wide moments ago.

Gritting my teeth, I open my eyes and start the whole process over again.

Ever since that kiss, I haven't been able to *not* notice Mira. Before, she was just Ramsey's little sister, the girl we had to watch out for when she followed us into the woods or needed help at school. I went through all of high school noticing girls, and never once saw Mira as anything more than my best friend's sister.

And then she kissed me.

I throw my duffel bag onto my bed, unzipping it harshly. Tossing old gym clothes I cleaned out of my office down the laundry chute, I pull out my maroon high-tops and spray them with some Febreze thing April gave me last time I saw her. The scent of cranberries wafts into the air, and I smile. April always buys everything cranberry scented she can find ever since Mira pitched the biggest, and only, fit I've ever seen her have at six years old. She went through a phase where she wanted everything to be red and freaked out when she realized red doesn't have a scent. So, April convinced her that cranberry is the scent of red and since then, April always buys things cranberry scented, probably inadvertently.

So, now my life smells red.

It took everything in me not to kiss her back at her party. When I asked her what she wanted for her birthday, I figured she'd ask for something simple. Mira rarely went for anything fancy other than paints or art supplies.

But I never imagined when I stepped closer to her, she'd crane up to kiss me. After I pulled away from the shock of it, my body screamed to go back in, but my brain caught up in time to stop me. She may have changed in my eyes, but she's still Ramsey's sister. Ramsey, the friend whose family took me in whenever I wandered over. The friend I can't lose. Not even for the girl who somehow transformed after one kiss.

I rip my shirt over my head, stalking into my bathroom,

knowing nothing but a cold shower will soothe my edgy nerves right now. A tent starts forming in my gym shorts, the way it always does when I dwell on that kiss too much. Turning on the faucets and stripping off my pants and boxers, I jump under the spray, hissing at the water. It hits the back of my neck and slides down. My abs contract and my semi deflates while I stare at the cobalt tiles in front of me. Resigned, I place my palms against them and count while I breathe.

There is no world where I get to kiss Mira back. Stopping myself was the only thing to do. Mira would never give up if she knew I wanted to kiss her back. She would have dug her heels in and made it impossible to ignore her, impossible for Ramsey to not sense something. And Ramsey would never allow anything to go on. Not with his little sister.

I have two options. Lose Ramsey and the Adams, the only people I consider family, in one fell swoop or keep my distance from Mira and keep Ramsey and the Adams in my life.

The rejected expression on Mira's face when I walked away from her on that wall flashes in my mind.

I put my head under the shower spray, letting it beat down and soak my hair. It falls in my eyes, water sliding down my shoulders and back.

The pain in her eyes causes the feral guilt in my stomach to gnaw. I hate seeing Mira in pain. Even as kids, I can remember holding her hand while Ramsey carried her into the house when she fell off her bike. I always wanted to make sure she was okay. So, putting that pain in her eyes when I told her she shouldn't have kissed me felt wrong.

That pain kept her from following me though. I needed

to get away from her and stay away and that pain acted as the barrier making it possible to do so.

The image of her next to my truck strikes again, and I feel myself start to get hard despite the cold water. Avoiding her was simple when we lived three hours away from each other and I only had to see her sporadically throughout the year. Now she lives five minutes away.

My dick certainly likes that idea. I shake my head, turning the warm tap completely off. The icy water does nothing but shallow my breathing further. Gripping my traitorous cock, I slide my fist fast, thinking about Cheryl at work today. She always overtly flirts with everybody which usually turns me off, but she wore a low cropped sports bra and leaned over the front desk when I came over to check on things.

Picturing her smirk and tits, I pump faster.

She came into my office an hour later to hand off some paperwork and I got to see her fit ass outlined almost obscenely in her spandex leggings when she turned and swayed her hips on the way out.

I let my head tip back and the image abruptly changes. Mira's flushed face and deep brown eyes stare up at me. My mind homes in on her slightly open mouth and focuses all my attention on her plump bottom lip, glossy and bitable. With a groan, my hips jerk forward as I come all over the tiles before I can stop myself.

My jaw tightens and I watch my cum wash down the wall with the beads of overspray coming off my skin. The fist not holding my deflating dick pulls back and slams into the tiles, pain radiating from my knuckles and momentarily spiking the leftover tingles of my orgasm. I punch the wall a few more times, letting go of my cock and using my other hand too. Once my breathing comes in harshly and my knuckles hurt enough, I lean my head against the tile and groan.

Ignoring her is going to be impossible and I'm not sure how long I'll hold out since she's already invading my mind.

Finishing my shower, I wander back downstairs, Smith now nowhere to be seen. Royal stares at the TV, trying to kill zombies with his guard, Lev. I walk past and head into the kitchen, grabbing a water bottle from the fridge and searching for something to eat, zoning out a bit.

"What happened to your hands?"

I jump, turning to find Smith nodding to the reddened knuckles of my left hand that rests on top of the counter.

I shut the fridge before answering. "Forgot to wrap them before I went in on the bag today."

Smith pauses, forehead pinching as he twists from side to side on a barstool. I decide to make a sandwich, setting out to grab the ingredients from around the kitchen.

"You won't be able to avoid Mira next week."

I control my reaction, scowling into a cabinet before closing it and turning back. "I don't know what you mean."

Smith and I have never talked about what he saw past the quick warning I threatened him with if Ramsey ever found out about it from him. Beyond the teasing he sometimes does, we never talk about it openly.

I lay out my sandwich ingredients and Smith stays silent long enough for me to think the conversation has dropped. But while I start assembling, he says, "Her party. Ramsey is throwing her birthday party here next week."

I frown.

Smith drums his knuckles against the countertop. "You can't exactly schedule yourself for an overnight shift, so you'll have to be here."

I continue making my food, not looking up at Smith

while I try to ignore what he said. I have mulled over this problem for the last couple weeks, ever since Ramsey decided he wanted to throw Mira an eighteenth birthday party. He had the idea when we were together, driving somewhere. I'd been talking him down while he vented about how much he wanted to say something to April about changing Mira's party this year, knowing Mira would be pissed if he did.

If she thinks something will hurt April, she refuses to do it, even if it means making herself uncomfortable.

Ramsey got frustrated to the point where he just blurted, "Might as well just throw her my own party." I stayed silent, but his eyes lit up and he sat forward in the truck. "Oh my god, *I'll* throw her a party." He immediately called her and put it on speaker, her voice coming through a moment later.

"What's up?"

"I'm throwing you your own party." His words rushed out of him, excitement making him practically giddy.

"What?"

"On your birthday. I'm throwing you a party. An actual party, not the big fancy shit Mom always throws." He practically bounced in his seat. "It'll be your first week at school, you can bring Bentley." He paused, the air seeming to deflate out of him. I smirked, knowing what he would say next. "And Autumn, if you want."

Mira's laugh poured through the phone. My hand flexed on the wheel.

"Gee, I can bring my best friends? Thanks so much, Ram."

Ramsey rolled his eyes at her response. "Shut up. It's going to be great. We'll have it at the house on the sixth."

"That's a Wednesday, Ram."

She sighed. I could hear it in her voice. She hated those balls April threw for her, but she refused to change them.

Adding a second party on top of that added more stress to the birthday she already hated.

"Yeah, I know, but it's your actual eighteenth." He waited but she never said anything. "Come on, bug. I'll take care of everything. All you have to do is show up."

Another sigh.

"Fine. I guess it'll be nice to have something to do that night."

I held back a snort, rubbing my free hand against my grinning mouth.

Ramsey fist pumped the air. "It'll be fun, I swear. I'll see you soon. Love you, bye." He didn't wait for her to respond, hanging up and already launching into what we would need and how many people he should tell. I nodded along, dread setting into my chest while he kept talking.

She will be in my house all night.

She came to see Ramsey several times over the last few years, but never stayed the night so leaving while she visited was easy enough.

But Smith has a point. There's no way to get out of being here for her birthday. Ramsey would notice and ask questions.

"You want me to run interference?" Smith leans forward, snagging the cheese slices and pulling them to his side of the island.

I wrinkle my brow at him.

"I can interrupt if you get stuck with Ramsey and her. Make excuses if he starts asking about where you are."

I put the knife down. "Why would you do that?"

Smith shoves a slice of cheese into his mouth. "Because I've watched you bend over backwards to stay away from her for two years. Be heartbreaking to see you lose all that in just one night." Food flies out of his mouth while he speaks.

I shake my head and finish my sandwich.

"Unless you don't want to stay away from her anymore?"

I look back up and find him smirking.

"She'll be eighteen next week. That's plenty old enough to make her own decisions."

I snort. "I didn't avoid her because I was scared of rejection."

Smith nods, shoving more cheese into his mouth. "He'd get over it eventually."

I shake my head, and he clicks his tongue.

"She's going to be around a lot more." He stands up and starts to walk away, throwing a last comment over his shoulder. "Guess you'll be spending more time at the gym."

I grip the island and roll my shoulders. Maybe taking on some more hours isn't such a bad idea.

4

After lunch, Mom insists on coming to see Bentley's room. We wave goodbye to Autumn and Aria, Mom, Bentley, and I heading up to the eighth floor. When the elevator doors open, we turn left and walk all of three feet before coming up on the open door of suite 815. Beside it sits some of the provided dorm furniture stacked haphazardly in the hall.

A board voice belonging to a tall olive toned guy reaches us first. "It's not that big of a deal, Gwen." He leans against the wall with his arms crossed over his chest, eyes sliding slowly to the three of us stopped in the doorway to Bentley's suite.

The layout inside has changed completely. New couches and side tables take up the majority of the room, the TV now mounted to the wall over an elaborate entertainment center. Trinkets and small touches litter the room, a circular mirror mounted to the wall between the bedroom doors across from us. The board guy leans beside it, now looking me up and down.

In the middle of everything stands my RA, Gwen, with

an older man who seems to be a mixed version of her and board guy who must be Bentley's roommate.

"It's like six building violations, Axel. And where did all the furniture go?" Gwen gestures around before noticing our arrival and quickly closing her mouth and lowering her hands.

"Hello." The man beside her steps toward us. "I'm Jack, Axel's father. And this is my daughter Gwen." He holds out his hand to Mom who steps forward and takes it hastily, staring up at him with a smile.

"I'm April Adams." She lets go of his hand, putting her arm around my shoulders. "This is my daughter Amiria and her best friend Bentley." She nods over to Bentley who puts his hands in his pockets.

"Mira is one of my freshmen, Dad." Gwen steps forward, her giant smile back in place. "I met her and Bentley this morning. I didn't realize you were Axel's roommate."

Board guy, Axel, raises his hand and gives a short wave before tucking it back in against his chest. He smirks at me, and I look away, finding his father smiling at my mother.

"Are you my RA too?" Bentley asks, ignoring the adults staring at each other. My eyes narrow at my mother's returning smile, but then she turns to Gwen.

Gwen shakes her head, a small laugh coming out. She, Bentley, and Axel talk, but I tune out, watching my mother glance over at Jack a few times while checking the suite out.

Bentley suddenly grabs my hand, pulling me toward one of the bedroom doors. Bursting in, we pause and find a complete replica of his bedroom back home, rock posters and all.

"Oh my god, they're monsters," I jibe.

Bentley tries to seem disappointed but can't wipe the smile off his face. "They're insane, that's for sure."

I nudge his shoulder. "You love it though."

He shrugs. We head back to the living room, finding Gwen admonishing Axel in a hushed tone. He has his arms crossed, barely paying attention. Mom speaks quietly with Jack, laughing at something he says. They all turn to us as we walk out.

"Everything in place?" Mom asks Bentley. He nods, ushering her to come see. She touches Jack's arm before walking with Bentley into his room. My stomach sours.

"Your mom didn't want to see you off on your first day?" I say to Axel, narrowing my eyes on Jack.

"Can't really see me off from six feet under," Axel deadpans.

His words slide through me with a sickly-sweet venom. My spine snaps straight, face falling. "I'm sorry. I didn't realize."

"It's okay," Gwen says, stepping around Axel who now stands at his full height and looks at me frigidly. She puts her hand on his shoulder, and he glances away from me. "She died years ago, it's just a bit fresh on days like today."

Jack puts his hands in his pockets. "I should probably say goodbye to Layla before I go."

"Are you walking out?" Mom asks, coming back into the room with her arm linked through Bentley's. Jack nods, a tinge of guilt in his eyes.

"I should probably start heading back as well." She releases Bentley's arm, giving him a hug before coming over and putting her hand on my cheek. "Have a great week, baby. I'll see you on Friday."

We hug and I swallow to alleviate my suddenly dry throat. She wipes the corner of my eyes quickly when we pull back and I smile. Stepping back, she looks at Jack. "I'll walk out with you."

He nods, clapping Axel on the back. "See you in a few weeks, son." Axel tips his chin once to his dad.

Gwen squeezes Axel's shoulder, before letting go. "I'll go with you to see Layla, Dad."

Jack nods and gestures for the two of them to go ahead. Mom waves one last time and the three of them walk out.

"I really am sorry. I shouldn't have asked about your mom like that," I say once we hear the elevator doors close behind them.

Axel shrugs. "It's fine. Dad wasn't exactly being subtle with your mom." He smirks and I bristle. "Guess it's fair for me to ask where your dad is now?"

Bentley crosses his arms, stepping a little bit between us. "Back off, dude."

I put my hand on his arm. "No, he's right, that's fair. He's in Helsinki. He has business all over the world so he travels a lot and couldn't make it with Mom today."

"So, they're still married," Axel muses. I clench my fist. "Didn't seem it a few minutes ago."

Bentley tenses under my hand.

Axel puts his hands up in surrender. "I just mean, she didn't warn Dad off and she wasn't wearing a ring."

My eyebrows knit as I try to remember if she wore it at lunch.

Bentley glances at me. "She probably just forgot it at home."

I nod, but my face won't smooth out. I can't remember if I saw her wearing it this summer.

"Want to go see if your roommate showed up?" Bentley smiles, his distraction tactic on full display.

I shrug then nod, bees invading my stomach. We got our roommate assignments at the start of summer with their cell numbers listed in the orientation packet. Once I read *Janette*

Davidson, I started envisioning how this year might go. Late night chats with piles of junk food, walking to class together, meeting up for meals and parties. Looking her up on socials, I found all her posts centered around her mom's political campaign and figured she was too busy to reach out first. Biting the bullet, I sent Janette a few messages introducing myself and asking about things I was bringing to check we didn't double up.

She never texted me back.

Bentley reasoned that they probably just gave me the wrong number and I tried to let the explanation settle, but my anxiety ran a bit wild with reasons she wouldn't respond.

Bentley invites Axel but he declines, needing to unpack and heading into his room. "He seems chill," Bentley says as we head out to the elevator. "I should probably go find Sean to get my keys. Meet you there?"

I nod, my stomach knotting. He walks off and I enter the elevator. As it sinks down to my suite, my stomach starts eating itself. I hate going into new situations alone.

The door to my suite still sits open, soft voices from inside drifting to me when I get closer.

"It's fine, Christopher. I don't care which room I'm in," a feminine voice implores.

"She should have waited for you to pick rooms together. It's just rude."

I turn the corner into the suite, finding the petite amber skinned girl I saw beaming on social media. Janette's hair is cinched into two tight buns on top of her head and she's moving things off a pile in the living room and into the vacant room beside mine. A man lounges on one of the sofas, feet hanging off the arm as he takes up most of the couch, staring at the ceiling.

I knock on the door, pulling both of their eyes toward me. Janette stops with a box in her hands, looking me over in the doorway.

"Hi, I'm Mira. You must be Janette." I walk further into the suite. My shoulders tense and I suddenly feel like I am intruding in my own space.

The man on the couch sits up. "I thought your roommate's name was Amy or something?"

"Amiria," Janette corrects, continuing into her room. She comes back a moment later, empty handed. "Do you shower in the morning?"

I look at the guy before looking back at her. "Um, usually."

"Perfect. I usually shower at night, and I really didn't want to have to change up my routine." She picks up another box and goes back into her room. The guy watches her ass the whole way.

"You could always just come back home with me, J. Keep your routine exactly how it's always been." The guy flashes her a smile when she pokes her head around the corner.

"Nice try, Chris," she scolds, but her breath seems to have left her lungs. "Mom already paid the tuition so there's no backing out now." She disappears again without taking another box.

"Do you want some help?" I step forward to pick up a table lamp, but Janette appears in a flurry and blocks me.

"No, it's okay," she says hurriedly. "It looked like you had plenty to unpack yourself."

I step back, heart hammering in my chest as I shuffle my feet. "Okay. Um, about that Keurig. I texted you to make sure—

"Don't worry about it," Janette says with a wave of her hand. She grabs the lamp off the pile. "I don't drink coffee.

The caffeine is really bad for you." She disappears into her room again.

My stomach drops as she confirms that she got my messages and just never sent anything back. I look over at Chris who flashes me a smarmy smile before laying back down on my couch. His eyes close and he bounces one of his feet, drumming his fingers on his chest.

Bentley appears in the doorway and my lungs expand. Glancing at Chris, he twirls his new keys around his finger. "All set. This your new roommate?" He walks over to me with a nod at Chris whose eyes fly open at the sound of Bentley's voice.

"No, that'd be me." Janette stands in her doorway, hands on her hips again. She takes him in from head to toe before openly sneering. "This your boyfriend?" She looks back at me.

I shake my head. "No, Bentley's just a friend." Chris sits up on the couch.

"You wound me," Bentley clutches his chest and I frown.

"You gay or something?" Chris asks, standing up. He falls a few inches shorter than Bentley who narrows his eyes. Chris puffs his chest almost comically.

"You have a problem with it if I was?" The guy has some mass on Bentley, but I can see that won't matter if he answers yes.

Chris deflates a bit, backing down. "No, just want to make sure you're not sniffing around my girl."

Janette snorts. "Babe, come on. This guy is not my type." She grabs some more stuff and continues moving.

"Don't worry," Bentley adds. "Snob isn't mine."

Chris's jaw slams audibly shut. He walks past Bentley, shoving into his shoulder on the way. "Stay away from Janette," he says before disappearing after her.

I grab Bentley's hand, pulling him into my room and closing the door.

"He's a fucking prick." Bentley sits down on my bed.

I nod. "She's not much better," I add, hoping the door and walls are thick enough to muffle our conversation. I twist the scarlet scrunchie at my wrist.

Bentley shrugs. "You're always welcome to my place when you need to get away." He grabs a box and starts taking things out and setting them up. I glance at the pile of dresser pieces on the floor and sigh. Today could have gone better.

5

My first week decides to follow suit. I get lost and show up late to two different classes on Monday. Someone accidentally spills food all over me in the dining hall on Wednesday. And Janette basically ignores me whenever we're in the dorm together, rarely responding to my attempts at conversation with anything more than one word.

I start finding excuses to escape the suite more often, avoiding interacting with her.

Friday starts out shit. I have my first chemistry lab at nine A.M., and it lasts the three full hours. We spend the first hour writing reports on lab safety before starting on neutralization of acids and bases. My partner doesn't help at all, only in this 101 chem course to satisfy the gen ed requirement like the majority of the students here. I get a text halfway through from Janette letting me know Chris showed up. So, after the lab ends, I wander around campus, avoiding my dorm.

Things finally brighten a bit when I go to my one art

class. I lose myself in the hour of drawing, everything around me finally melting away.

I feel lighter after, running back to my suite to grab my duffel and meet everyone downstairs. Autumn bounces on the sidewalk outside West Tower and we wait for Bentley. He said to specifically meet him outside instead of in the dorm's lobby.

A limo pulls up, grabbing the attention of a few people walking by. The back door pops open and Bentley springs out. "Surprise!" he yells.

I roll my eyes and Autumn actually jumps up and down.

"Curtesy of good ole Mom and Dad." He taps his knuckles on the top of the limousine. "We wouldn't all fit comfortably in Sadie." Sadie sits a few rows back in the parking lot, a shiny new Mercedes his grandfather gifted him for graduation.

"When you said you wanted to handle transportation, I assumed you'd just rent a van." Autumn slides into the backseat and I follow, handing my duffel off to the driver who appears in a suit to collect our bags. Bentley tsks at me, shaking his head as I get in.

"Nothing but the best for the birthday girl, Mir." He slides in, and the door closes. The inside is spacious with wrap around seating and a small bar along the left side.

"We're picking up Ramsey and Tanner as well," Bentley says when the limo pulls away from the curb and starts to leave campus.

Autumn explores the interior as we ride to the Ravens' mansion. Bentley fiddles with the Bluetooth settings on a screen in the back to try to get the playlist he apparently prepared for us to play. The limo stops outside the stone steps of the guys' house, and we slide down to make room. I end up beside Bentley facing backwards while Autumn sits against the right-hand side.

My brother emerges first; his messenger bag slung over one shoulder. Tanner follows with a duffel and right behind them comes Harley. My breath catches and Bentley and Autumn glance at me before looking back at the boys.

Ramsey slides in with a sly smile. "Traveling in style as per usual, Marshall." He fist bumps Bentley before settling down. He stiffens when he realizes he ended up next to Autumn and I hold my breath, hoping they don't get into it right away. "Ready for this weekend, sis?" He speaks across Autumn who toys with the edge of her skirt and stares ahead. I nod when Tanner slides in beside Ramsey, filling the capacity for the side of the limo. Harley gets in last and sits on the two-seater end exactly across from me before closing the door.

His eyes find mine when he settles back and I glance away, watching out the window as the driver gets back into the car. My heart feels like it's in my throat, attempting to escape my body entirely as it beats an unsteady rhythm through my veins.

Bentley puts his hand on my knee and squeezes. "You actually deciding to show up to one of these again, Sanders?"

I look back over at Harley, his posture tense as he answers Bentley. "Nah, just hitching a ride. My parents couldn't get me out of some function where they need to appear the perfect nuclear family."

Bentley nods and I look back out the window, my stomach lurching with disappointment. I scold myself. Harley made his feelings plenty clear over the last three years, so I don't know why I still react to him like this.

Bentley goes back to fiddling with the sound system,

pulling Tanner into the mix which allows Ramsey to move seats over next to Harley. Harley stares out the window as we get onto the highway and once the music starts playing, everyone chats and jokes about the shitshow this weekend will probably be. Tanner starts telling Autumn about my twelfth, the first time Mom got me to wear heels, when I accidentally tripped into the cake.

I tune out, studying Harley's profile for a moment, before glancing around to make sure no one noticed. Ramsey laughs loudly, making Autumn jump a little and Bentley adds a new story to the mix. With them all occupied, I let myself relax, closing my eyes.

My thoughts instantly return to the man ignoring me on the other side of the limo. I only met Harley's parents once in the past. We never hung out at his house unless they weren't home, and he never really spoke of them much. His housekeeper made most of the meals we ate there, and I got the sense as a kid that it was just the two of them a lot. Made sense that he would want to spend most of his time at our house.

Ramsey told me his parents had a cow when he dropped out of college. I wonder what kind of function two socialites would need their son at for good optics. Probably a charity event or something. Guess that means no random gift off Mom's registry this year.

I grin at the thought.

"You looking forward to your actual party on Wednesday?" Ramsey asks and my eyes open.

Grey eyes stare into mine from across the limo before turning to go back to looking out the window. I watch Harley for a moment, convincing myself that wasn't a mirage, and he actually had been staring at me when my eyes were closed.

"Another party?" Autumn's eyes practically bug out of her head.

"This one will be way more casual," Ramsey assures eyes never leaving my face. "No ball gowns required."

I laugh and Tanner shakes his head. "I think he's more excited for this than you are," he says to me.

"Always was," I say.

"Aw, come on, Mira! It's going to be your first real birthday party. Get excited," Ramsey whines.

"Oh, I'm excited. Just not jumping for joy level. Still have to make it through tomorrow night before I can look forward to Wednesday."

We all laugh and as it dies down, Bentley pipes up. "You going to be at Mira's actual birthday party, Harley?"

I cut Bentley a look, but he simply smiles innocently back.

Harley turns back from the window to catch the exchange and I feel my face flush crimson.

"Yeah, I'll be there," he says, watching me.

"Of course, he'll be there," Ramsey adds, looping an arm around Harley's neck. "None of us would miss Mira's first college party." Harley shoves Ramsey off, punching him lightly in the ribs once free.

Conversation flows again and I glance back at Harley, finding his eyes already on me. I startle and look away again, nearly missing the ghost of a smile that seems to play at the edge of his lips.

We pull up outside my childhood home and I breathe more evenly. Mom opens the oak door and rushes down the steps with a shriek.

"I missed you two," she yells, crushing me in a hug.

"Seems like you missed someone a bit more," Ramsey mutters, and Mom reaches out and swats him. She lets me go and takes his shoulders.

"You come and go more often, mister. This is the first time your sister has been so far from home." She hugs him before moving on to hug Harley. He beams down at her as she lets go, patting his cheek before grabbing Autumn up next.

We all move into the house, already being set up for the party.

Autumn chuckles. "I always forget how big this place is without all the furniture." She shakes her head at the checkerboard dance floor already set up in the middle.

Ramsey throws an arm around my shoulders. "Yes, well father does like his five-digit square footage."

Mom admonishes him before turning to Autumn. "Don't worry, dear, I'm still not fully used to all this grandeur either." Ramsey and I make a face at each other behind her back. We may not have started out wealthy, but Mom has some expensive tastes at times.

"Home away from home," Harley murmurs. Mom reaches out and squeezes his hand, glowing.

I glance at her hand, suddenly remembering what Axel said last week, and finding nothing on any of her fingers. I check her necklace, a simple silver pendant on a chain. A frown pulls at my mouth, and I fiddle with the scarlet satin scrunchie on my wrist.

Mom looks over us all before ushering everyone into the kitchen for food. We fill up the stools at the kitchen island and Mom listens eagerly as we all tell her about our first weeks. Ramsey complains about the professor he TA's for this year already starting to lean on him.

I sip the hot chocolate Mom placed in front of each of us. Mine has extra whipped cream and chocolate shavings, the familiarity warming me twofold.

Harley sits beside Ramsey and when it gets to his turn, Mom simply asks, "How's work?"

"Good," he nods. I take the opportunity to openly study him as he speaks. "Things are picking up now that people are back at school. We always have a huge increase in memberships right at the beginning of the school year, but half usually cancel before October so we'll see how it goes." He has a spark in his eyes when he talks about his job, and he seems to grin whenever he gets to tell Mom about it. He always loved being around Mom and she loved taking care of anyone who showed up at the door with us.

Mom nods. "That's great!" She brings over the platter of sandwich fixings. "What about you, baby?" She folds her hands on the island as she leans beside me, turning to fully face me while everyone scrambles to get bread, meats, and cheeses.

I give her a shortened rundown of my week, skipping anything about Janette and joking about getting lost.

"How are you liking the classes?"

I shrug, reaching forward to grab a roll. "It's syllabus week so we really haven't started doing much. I had my first lab this morning. It was cool I guess." Mom stares at me for a moment, seeming to read into what I'm not saying, but smiles nonetheless.

"Oh," she says, jumping up. "I forgot the chips." She rushes back to the pantry, coming out with three different bags and placing them on the table. As she takes her seat again, she grins. "Your dress got here this morning."

I swallow the bite in my mouth and return her grin.

"Great. I'll try it on after this." Mom nods and asks Autumn how her classes are going.

Ramsey's eyes meet mine and one side of his mouth pulls up as pity oozes toward me. I nod. Only a little over twenty-four hours till I can relax and enjoy being home for a bit.

The party noise quiets as I step out onto the patio in my blood red dress. I finally worked up the nerve to request red for my eighteenth and for the first time I didn't feel like shredding the gown the second I saw it.

I walk over to the corner of the patio, leaning against the wall like I did the last two years, visiting the spot where my most vivid dreams take place. In my sleep, Harley pulls me closer instead of pushing me away and things heat up from there. My subconscious usually draws from my past sexual experiences, slotting Harley in over someone else. I close my eyes, imagining how different that night could have been.

I have never regretted kissing Harley; it was what I wanted. But my imagination can't help trying to change the past and as a glutton for punishment, I always seek out these stolen moments to play pretend for a minute or two.

Rustling in the woods pulls my face to the side as my eyes fly open and a spike of fear shoots through me. Harley walks out of the trees, glaring at the ground, shoulders tense, clad in a black suit minus the jacket. I freeze, my heart pounding loud enough that I think the sound will give away my location. He makes it up three of the five stairs before glancing over the patio. He startles when he sees me, standing in the exact spot of the botched kiss two years prior.

Moments pass as my heart thunders on, and I swallow when he takes in my gown and decorated updo. Grey eyes settle back on mine and the look he wears makes me warm.

"Got kicked out again." His voice stays low. "Started an argument at dinner so hopefully that'll be the last time I have to go over there." He climbs the last two stairs, stopping once more when we are on level ground.

My brain races for a response, coming up empty every corner it turns.

"Going to go crash in one of the guest rooms. If your mom asks, tell her I'll talk about it tomorrow."

I nod and he does another sweep over me before heading toward the back doors.

Opening one and starting to step through, he pauses. Glancing at me again, he deadpans, "Nice dress," before disappearing inside.

I wait a full minute, counting in my head before moving away from the wall and clutching my chest. My pulse thumps erratically, and I shake my head.

Harley just spoke to me. Willingly. With no one else around.

After he caught me reminiscing about our first kiss.

I close my eyes.

The door opens again, and party noise filters out. I glance up to see Bentley poking out. "Mir, we've been looking everywhere for you, come on." He waves me forward and my legs mechanically follow. "Tanner said he brought your gift from Smith, so God knows what that'll be."

I glance back at the patio corner before heading inside, wondering if my brain finally snapped and I hallucinated the last few minutes.

6

Harley

I tip the cup, downing the rest of my beer as Mira walks into my house. People already mill around, drinking, shouting, and playing games throughout the open first floor space. Parties at our place have become ritualistic at the Coast, everyone trying to find out when one happens so they can show up and say they've been. I usually like the opportunity to find someone to hook up with or challenge Smith to a drinking contest but getting ready tonight felt somber. I can't risk drinking too much, but as the time dwindled down to her arrival, I snagged a drink to try to settle my jumpy nerves.

She drowns everything out around her. Her thick brown hair falls over her shoulders and down her back in loose waves and I clench my fist as the thought of walking over and running my fingers through it crosses my mind. Her outfit is simple, but screams Mira, the oversized faded red flannel around her shoulders having once been her father's. She walks more confidently in her black converse tonight than in the maroon heels on Saturday and she holds her head high, the black choker at her neck displaying a small silver pendant that shines even in the dim lighting. She wears a giant smile as she steps into the house, peeking around at everything happening.

I've watched her descend the monumental staircase at the Adams' house at least a dozen times in a multitude of poofy gowns and never saw her smile this big on any of those occasions. The corners of my mouth lift while I watch her take it all in.

Bentley and Autumn follow, the new goth chick with them as well. They each pause in the threshold and glance around, Marshall grinning while the girls marvel. Ramsey walks up, Royal and Tanner at his heels. I hear him greeting them, hugging his sister, and punching Marshall for some comment. Royal hugs her next, whispering in her ear and making me tense. I grab another beer off the counter beside me and walk briskly over to the group. Tanner moves in once Royal detaches himself from Mira. My usually aloof friend eyes the new girl at the back of the pack for a moment too long. I sidle up next to Ramsey who watches Mira and grins. He glances over, double taking when he notices me.

Tanner steps back, and Smith swoops in from the shadows with a loud, "Happy birthday Mira-cakes!" before lifting her off her feet and twirling her around. When he sets her back down, he leans back only to kiss her on both cheeks. I stop myself from crushing the red solo cup in my hand and glare at him as he winks over his shoulder. Ramsey growls, assuming the wink is for him, and pries his hands off her shoulders. Mira giggles at the whole thing, thanking him while I suppress a groan. Smith doesn't need more encouragement.

"Hands off the birthday girl, Reznikov. You're lucky I even let you attend." Ramsey steers him to the back of the group beside me before letting him go. "You going to say happy birthday to my sister, Har?"

I look away from Mira to glance at Ramsey before turning back to find big brown eyes staring up at me. She snags her bottom lip with her teeth, and I follow the movement before averting back to her eyes and saying, "Happy birthday, Meerkat."

Her mouth pops open at the accidental use of her nickname, but she recovers quickly, thanking me with the biggest smile I've seen so far tonight. I hastily take a sip of my beer to stop myself from reciprocating and nod before glancing away.

Smith smirks at me before Marshall tries to get everyone to sing happy birthday much to Mira's mortification.

"Stop it!" She covers his mouth with her hand. "I don't want people knowing it's my birthday." I turn back to her, all of us focused on Mira now. She looks at everyone in the group. "I want this to just be a party. We can know it's for me, but I want one birthday where no one in the room is clamoring to fake pleasantries with me so they can get closer to the people in my life." She gives each of my friends a pointed look, ending with Ramsey.

He nods. "You got it, bug." He puts an arm around her shoulders, pulling her away from the doorway and into the house. I watch them walk away, sipping the beer more.

"And the fun begins," Smith whispers to me before following them with Bentley, Autumn, and the goth girl.

I wander the house as the party seems to happen around me. I can't settle in for long without finding the guest of honor nearby. I actively try not to seek her out, yet find myself near her or hearing her voice, her laugh and it pulls my attention over to her. I throw the idea of not drinking out the window and join a game of flip cup to try to avoid Mira.

Maybe if I don't move for a minute, I won't end up in the same space as her. Smith does well running interference for a bit, but he started the night taking something, so it isn't long before he abandons his duties to make out with some blonde before leading her up to his room. The game gets tense, coming down to me and Tanner going head-to-head on the last flip, but I manage to land mine a second before he does. Everyone on my side of the table screams, the girl beside Royal taking the opportunity to rub against him as we celebrate. I gloat over Tanner, who nods good naturedly, before looking around the room and landing in Mira's gaze.

I freeze, our eyes locking from where she sits on the back of the comfy chair Bentley occupies across the room. She smiles and tips her head toward me and the game before breaking the eye contact to join the conversation around her. I watch her lean forward and say something over Marshall's shoulder that makes Autumn tip her head back and cackle. She grins, sitting back up as Marshall turns and feigns hurt which she sticks her tongue out at.

"Anyone bothering her tonight?" Ramsey appears at my side, watching his sister with me. I shake my head, trying to clear the haze I've gained over the last hour or so.

"Nah, she's just been hanging out with Marshall, Autumn, and that new girl."

"Good." Ramsey nods. "She looks like she's having a good time, right?" I suddenly realize how nervous he is to disappoint Mira.

"She looks happy, dude," I say, staring at her. "She never looks this light at your mom's parties."

Ramsey grins and claps me on the back. "She does look happy, doesn't she." We watch her have a good time with her friends for a bit before I turn away, something slithering in my chest.

"Surprised you let Autumn in the front door." I chuckle as Ramsey scowls at the girl across the room. I put a hand on his shoulder, and he shrugs it off.

"Tonight's about Mira, not me," he says, disgruntled.

I nod, glancing back at Mira who leans back to talk to two girls behind the group. I watch, her smile now gone, though she doesn't seem actively upset. The way she leans back pulls the tank top under her flannel up and a strip of skin shows above the waistband of her jeans. I stare, my mouth going a bit slack.

"Whose Harley checking out?" Smith slams into me as he tries to nudge my shoulder. Ramsey catches him before he tips forward.

"He's watching out for Mira," Ramsey says with a grunt, righting Smith on his feet, still swaying a bit. "Making sure no one drunk bothers her." Ramsey looks pointedly at Smith who sloppily tries to smirk.

"Oh please." He snorts. "Like we haven't all checked out Mira at some point."

My hand twitches, but Ramsey beats me to it, slapping the back of Smith's head. "You better not have."

Smith tries to defend himself and Ramsey shouts back, Royal walking up to referee. He hands me his beer as he steps in. I glance back to find the area Mira and her friends had been now vacant. I search around but can't find them and close my eyes, reminding myself I'm not supposed to be looking for her.

I pour Royal's beer down my throat before opening my eyes and hunting for something to distract me.

7

Autumn leans back and cackles after I tell Bentley he has no chance with a girl in the corner.

He turns and pouts. "You have no faith in me?"

Aria chuckles.

"No, I've just seen her touch that guy's arm like three times." I nod over at her as she does it again and Bentley watches before scowling. He slouches and I pat his back before sipping the drink he snuck me when Ramsey was distracted across the room.

I tried to pour myself one when we first got to the house, but my brother swooped in, taking the cup from my hands, and reprimanding me for underage drinking. I know for a fact he didn't wait till twenty-one to drink so once his back was turned, Bentley passed me a cup and I strategically hid it. I have a nice buzz, the feeling good and drowning out the effects of the adrenaline spike I got when Harley wished me happy birthday.

I feel the most comfortable I ever have on my birthday. Partially thanks to Ramsey, but also from that small moment of Harley's attention. Things feel like they're changing back. Maybe we can be friends again.

Someone taps me on the shoulder, and I turn, leaning back to see Gwen beaming down at me. "Hey, great party! And happy birthday! I stopped by your suite earlier, but Janette told me you were out. Figured I'd stop by. I've never been to one of the guys' parties." A girl with the same skin tone as Gwen stands off to the side, hands in the pockets of her jean jacket while she glances around unimpressed. Janette stands sheepishly next to her.

I nod, thanking Gwen as the girl beside her lolls her head toward me. Her hair is shoulder length, dyed black at the roots and an unnaturally bright auburn at the ends. Her eyebrows are light under her bangs though, the color matching Gwen's hair.

"Leave her alone, Gwenivere." Tanner appears behind the couch Autumn and Aria sit on, eyes shrouded in the low lighting. Gwen takes a step back and I lean back too far, losing my balance. Aria leans forward and grabs my arm, pulling me back when my head rushes. Gwen puts her hands on my shoulders to steady me and I tip my head back to thank her.

"You need water," she says, ushering me off the back of the chair and toward the kitchen. Everyone else follows, Tanner standing beside me and glaring at Gwen while she pours water from the Brita. Janette leans against the island next to Bentley while the other girl with them leans away from the group beside her. Gwen hands me the water, looking over at the girl, who surveys the room. "This is my sister, Layla," Gwen says, pulling her sister over. She presses her mouth into a line and glances around.

"Mira," I say, sounding too loud. "Nice to meet you."

"Okay, she got her water. Time to go, Gwenivere," Tanner

says, stepping forward. I step between them, leaning back against Tanner.

"It's okay, Tan. She's not bothering me."

He peers down at me and raises an unimpressed eyebrow. "Don't let Ramsey see you getting drunk." He walks away after the warning, disappearing in the random mass of people around the room. I lean against the kitchen counter, gulping my water. Everyone watches at me as I do, making me put the glass down after guzzling half.

"This is Autumn and Aria," I point at the girls in turn. "They're freshman on the second floor at West Tower." Gwen turns toward them, asking how they like Keith as their RA. I sigh when they start up a conversation, taking another sip of water. Bentley watches me from beside Janette who stands with her arms folded, pointedly only looking at Gwen.

"Nicely done," Layla whispers, standing beside me while her sister moves closer to the other two. "She's a bloodhound." I raise a questioning brow at her, and she leans in closer. "Hard to distract when she's got the scent." She smirks, and I laugh.

"You go to the Coast?" I ask.

Layla nods. "Liberal arts for right now. I'm trying to figure out what I want to do, and dear old dad didn't want me just lazing around the house while my brother and sister got degrees." She shrugs, widening her arms with her hands in her jacket pockets still. "At least now I have J here to keep me company." She sneers at Janette who flips her off.

"Ease up, Little Miss Sunshine. Try being fun." Bentley knocks into her, probably a little harder than he would if sober.

She glares at him. "I am fun." I snort before I can stop

myself and even Layla snickers lightly. Janette turns her glare to Layla.

She shrugs, only half attempting to stop smiling. "Come on, J. You haven't even had a drink since we got here."

Janette's arms unfold and she searches around, determination crinkling her forehead. She locates a nearby half empty bottle of clear liquor. Giving each of us a pointed glance, she uncaps the bottle, taking a swig and grimacing once she lowers it back down. "Fun enough for you?" She sneers at Bentley.

He laughs, walking over to the fridge and grabbing a jug of juice from the door while she finds a cup and pours the liquor straight into it.

"Why don't we try mixing it with something," he says as he takes the cup from her hands, pouring the juice in over the alcohol. She grabs it back from him, and takes a large gulp, not making a face this time. Layla chuckles, grabbing herself a cup and handing it to Bentley. He mixes her a drink as well. I realize I need to pee and let Bentley know I'll be back. He nods, threatening to come after me if I take longer than ten minutes.

I wander upstairs, knowing where Ramsey's bathroom is and only stumbling a bit on the staircase. Someone stops me from falling and I throw out a *thank you* before continuing. At the top, I peer down the hall, seeing people talking and making out against the walls between me and the bathroom door. I start toward it, trying hard not to bump into anyone as I squeeze past them. Most of the guys' doors are closed but one sits open next to the bathroom. I glance in when I sidestep two men eating each other's faces against the wall.

The sight of a dark-haired girl straddling Harley on a bed as he kisses down her neck, hands moving under her shirt, stops me in my tracks. My stomach turns, and an ache spreads through my chest. The girl pulls Harley's face up to her own, the two kissing deeply.

I turn away, rushing into the bathroom next door and puking into the tub before I can make it to the toilet. Once I heave a couple of times, I stand, turning the shower on and rinse the tub before heading to the sink and rinsing my mouth.

My mind feels much clearer as I stand and focus on myself in the mirror. My eyeliner is smudged, eyes bloodshot, probably from the mix of alcohol and puking. My hair has a few mussed-up areas that I smooth with my fingers. I stare into my eyes, willing the tears pooling at my waterline to evaporate. When one falls down my cheek, I let go, letting myself cry for a minute before pulling it together and grabbing a wad of toilet paper to dry my cheeks. After blowing my nose, I pee quickly and wash my hands, walking back out and down the hall without looking anywhere but forward. Once I make it back to the first floor, I seek out Bentley, finding him leaning against a post under the stairs with Layla as they watch Janette dance on top of the kitchen island.

"Is she okay?" I ask, unsure how we got here while I was upstairs.

"She's proving she can be fun," Bentley murmurs. He glances over at me before doubling back. "What's wrong?"

Great, so my quick touch up did nothing to hide the quick crying jag. I wave him off. "I'm fine, just getting a little tired."

He nods. "Lemme grab Janette and we can all head back." I look over at Janette, now joined with a few other people on top of the island and laughing with her head thrown back. Autumn stands by the wall, talking animatedly with Gwen, while Aria plays with the lip of a cup and smiles at the guy talking to her.

"Nah, it's fine. You should probably keep an eye on Miss Fun over there. I can make it back on my own." He starts to protest, standing to full height and swaying a bit in the process. "It's fine, Bent. It's not even a ten-minute walk. I'll have my cell on me the whole time."

Bentley opens his mouth again, but the crowd behind me suddenly gasps together and we glance back to see Janette pitching to the side. Bentley rushes forward to catch her, Janette giggling in his arms once she lands. Bentley glances back at me while Janette struggles to free herself and I hold my phone up, pointing. "I'll text you when I get back to West Tower," I shout. He nods before turning back to Janette.

Layla gives me a one-handed salute and shouts, "Happy birthday," over the noise. I nod and walk toward the front door, glancing around for Ramsey or one of the guys. Seeing no one familiar, I slip out and start across the lawn toward campus. I text Ramsey to let him know I left and put my hands in my pockets as I walk. The streets are well lit from here to campus and the temperature hasn't fully dropped into fall so the air is cool but not chilly. I find it refreshing to walk away from all the noise and breathe in the cool night.

My brain keeps replaying the image of Harley under that girl. Then his words when I arrived play over the images. I sniffle back the onslaught of crying I'll let loose when I make it back to my dorm. I saw Harley date girls in high school, even know he isn't a virgin from the way he and Ramsey sometimes joke but seeing it firsthand in front of me is a whole new pain.

Suddenly the stupid kiss I managed to steal in tenth grade feels meaningless.

And that ache that started in my chest blossoms outward. He pushed me away every chance he got and here I am holding onto some dumb little crush, pining for a guy who spent a lot of time trying to avoid me. I feel pathetic, a few more tears leaking out without my permission. I hold the rest back, needing to see the street signs to make sure I turn when I need to and don't get lost.

Steps suddenly register in my ears and the hairs on the back of my neck stand up as I realize they're behind me on the sidewalk. I glance around, seeing a figure on the same side of the street as me a yard or two back. Needing to be on the other side when I turn, I cross the street and listen. A few moments later, I hear the footsteps follow me across the road.

Blood pounds in my ears, seeming to amplify the sounds of the steps as if they are gaining on me. I speed up, hearing the footsteps follow suit. I'm two streets away from Ring Road, but still another three-minute walk from there to West Tower. I grip my phone in my pocket, peeking over my shoulder to see that the figure still follows me, closer now. Facing forward, I decide the person is definitely male and definitely bigger than me, though they have their head down and wear baggy clothes.

My palms start to sweat while my stomach drops and without thinking, I take off in a dead sprint toward Ring Road. Unable to hear anything other than my own harsh breaths and the patter of my converse slapping the cement, I push myself down the street, making a wide turn onto Ring Road and watch West Tower come closer as I run. My mind races as images of a hand grabbing my shoulder and yanking me from behind keeps chills running up and down my spine. Finally, outside the door, I pull out my key ring, swiping my access card and pushing the door open the second the light turns green. Slamming the door behind me, I stare through the glass into the night.

No one stands in the streetlights on the road I just came from. I study the shadows, looking for any sign of movement. Panting, my breath starts to fog the glass in front of my face, and I step back, still frantically searching outside for the figure I felt chasing me. After minutes go by without anyone there, I jump at the sound of my phone vibrating. I pull it out of my pocket, seeing a text from Bentley asking if I made it.

I open the message, my fingers hovering over the keyboard. With another check around the view outside, I type back.

Made it back. See you tomorrow.

BENTLEY

👍👍👍

I put my phone back in my pocket, heading for the elevator.

I still feel spooked when I make it to the suite, double checking the lock before getting ready for bed. While I brush my teeth, I google self-defense courses in the area, finding a local gym that holds women's safety classes every other Friday. The next one is in two days, so I click the registration button and sign up, getting confirmation of my spot for the five o'clock class this Friday. I turn off my phone and get into bed, the events of the last few hours swirling in my system.

8

Harley

I pull the rolled-up mats out of the storage room with Sonya. People work out all over the gym tonight, early evening on a Friday being one of our busier times as people get out of class and get a workout in before going out for the night. Mornings are our busiest time, but the gym pretty much fills up until seven when numbers trail off and we start cleaning everything. I lift a mat on one end, Sonya taking the other. I smile and nod to a few of the regulars I know as we move to the training room.

Sonya chuckles when we throw the mat down. "Don't let Cheryl see you flirting with any of the customers. Their memberships will randomly get canceled."

I hum and roll my eyes, heading back out to the main room to get the rest of the mats.

We transport the other three, unrolling and arranging them for the class coming up. I grab the broom; brushing them off while Sonya starts stretching a bit.

"There are a few people already here for tonight's class. Do you want me to send them in?"

I turn to find Cheryl in the doorway, arms behind her

back and chest pushed out. Sonya coughs to hide another chuckle.

"Sure. Let Derek know to come join once his one on one is done." I turn my back to the door again while Cheryl bounces a little on her feet. She started working here last semester and she's the best one for greeting and signing up new members, but her over-the-top flirting grates on my nerves. If we weren't already down a trainer, I would look into replacing her.

Sonya stands up and greets the woman walking in. I put the broom away, coming back to see several more women joining the group around the edge of the mats. Sonya takes names, checking them off on the clipboard and I start stretching.

Tonight is a full class. The women's self-defense ones usually fill up at the beginning of the school year as freshman come in and decide to take it now that they live on their own. I hate how necessary this training often is but am all too happy to help as many women as possible feel safe and confident in their bodies offering a class like this. We always recommend taking it a few times to really get the muscle movements down without having to think about them in the moment.

Finishing my stretches, I introduce myself to the small group of women sitting near me. We start chatting about why they chose the class and how they like the gym, each of them blushing a bit as I nod and listen. I excuse myself when Derek walks in, throwing his water bottle and keys off to the side.

"Ready to get the shit kicked out of you?" Derek jokes, slapping my hand and giving me a half hug.

I nod and smirk. He starts to stretch, and I face the room,

taking my spot on the wall to observe the first part of the course while Sonya does the instruction.

My eyes instantly find the back of Mira's head, her dark hair double braided down her back as she sits cross-legged on the outskirts of the mat a few feet in front of me. She starts talking to the girl beside her who introduces herself and I stare at her profile, fists clenched as I try to think of an excuse to get out of the class. Mira smiles and her eyes pull to the side, finding mine where I restrain myself. She turns away quickly, glancing back over her shoulder for a second peek a moment later. Her eyes flash and her jaw ticks before she faces forward again.

My gut clenches.

Anger rolled off her toward me. She's mad I'm here?

Fuck. The gym has always been my place to get away from Mira when she came to visit. It was easy to schedule myself more hours or stay late doing admin work. But the idea that she could show up as a member once she lived here never even crossed my mind. I've never seen Mira in a gym before; didn't even know she owned the workout leggings she wears right now. She used to complain about gym in school and scoff whenever Ramsey invited her to join our football workouts. So, her sitting here in my gym was never a relative possibility.

Sonya starts the class as Derek stands and walks over to close the door to the main part of the gym. I force myself to stare at the wall across from me, ignoring the room while I try to figure out a way to get out of this. If there were another male trainer on tonight, I could switch out with them, but the only other two certified trainers tonight are Cheryl and Cat. They need a second guy for a full class to split the women up and run attack simulation drills. I take some deep breaths, settling into the fact that I can't leave. I just need to make sure Mira isn't in my group when Sonya splits them. At least Mira sat with her back to me. I can easily watch Sonya and avoid staring at her this way.

"There are a lot of reasons women sign up for this class," Sonya says, when I tune back in. She has run this class for the last two years and I helped with enough of them to know this speech already. "I volunteered to get trained for this after taking a self-defense course myself and I have heard a lot of different stories over the years. Most of them make me pissed we need these courses, but I'm also really happy that we offer them here by the college." She paces as she speaks.

I glance around at the different women, my eyes gravitating to Mira after a few swipes. Why is she here? The back of my neck prickles as I realize there must be a reason for her to sign up for the class. Did something happen? I don't look away from the back of her head until Sonya calls my name.

"Harley? Want to come help me show these ladies what they'll be learning tonight?"

I push off the wall, crossing between Mira and the girl beside her to enter the mats. Both lean away from me as I pass, and I ignore the pang in my stomach as I approach Sonya. She starts setting up the first scenario, placing herself in front of me. I grab her wrist and try to pull her into me. She counters with the first move of the night, effectively releasing herself and pushing me away. I study Mira's face as we go through the scenario again, slower so that the women can see how Sonya executes the move. She follows Sonya's movements with her eyes, never once looking at me beyond my hand. Her jaw stays clenched, and heat rises on her face, painting her cheeks ruby. I can practically see the anger radiating off her and for a moment my heart sinks as I wonder if I have something to do with the reason she is here tonight. But images of our very brief interactions over the last few weeks quickly follow that thought. No, something bigger must have happened.

Sonya and I go through the other four scenarios the women will be learning before she has them all stand up and pair off to practice the first one. I return to the wall beside Derek to wait for the next time when we'll both be needed.

"Who is she?" Derek nods to Mira, practicing the wrist move.

"My friend's sister," I reply, watching her falter a few times before landing it. She does it two more times correctly before Sonya calls for them to switch.

"She's hot," Derek says.

White hot anger burns through my chest. I glare at him. "We're teaching these women self-defense, Derek. If you make any one of them uncomfortable tonight, you will leave, and I will start looking for your replacement."

He holds his hands up, standing straighter. "Sorry man. I didn't mean anything by it." I stare him down for a few more moments before nodding once. He stares at his shoes after that.

I cross my arms and survey the class, checking in on how Mira does with the moves each time they change to a new one. She learns quickly, usually getting in a few practices after correctly executing them. I smile when she nails the last one, landing her partner on the ground. She breathes harshly but stares down at the woman in triumph. After helping her partner up, they switch and Mira becomes the attacker, helping the other woman learn the move when she can't quite get it right.

Sonya claps a few minutes later, and I straighten as she

explains that they will now be taking turns using the moves on Derek and me. She pats my chest when I stand beside her, assuring the women that Derek and I will be holding nothing back, but also help make corrections if needed. I glance at Mira, noticing her fists clench before she huffs a breath and looks away.

"Line up on that side of the room, two lines of ten." Sonya walks over to her bag and grabs a water bottle while the women line up. I watch Mira purposely cross the room to be in the line on Derek's side and my stomach tightens.

"Switch sides with me," I whisper quickly before informing the women that we will run through the first scenario a few times. "Once you have completed the move, head to the back of the line. Everyone will get a few shots at each of us."

Nodding to the first woman, I walk up and grab her wrist. I repeat the scenario four times before Mira stands in front of me.

Holding my breath as I grab her wrist, she immediately preforms the counter move perfectly though much more forcefully than the others. I give her an encouraging smile and she glares back. Turning on her heel, she heads to the back of the line.

The pattern continues, Mira giving me her all each time we face off. The third time she turns away, I call out, "Widen your stance a bit more before you swing your shoulder. It will give you a better anchor." She glowers back at me, returning the critique with a curt nod.

We run through the rest of the scenarios, with Mira overexerting herself each time she comes up against me. On the last one, she manages to put me on my ass all four times. I grin up at her on the last one, proud she was able to manage it since I tried my best not to let her and she looks exhausted. She huffs over me, strands of hair sticking to her forehead and poking out of her braids. All the breath seems to leave my body as we stare at each other for a moment. Then without a word, she walks to the back of the group, leaving me laid out on the mat.

I sit up as Sonya calls the women back to the center of the room. This last part is more about them getting their aggression out, but enough women commented about it being one of their favorite parts, so I don't mind donning the full body padding suit we purchased for this exact use.

Derek and I, clad in bulky safety foam, stand on the mats as the women line up again, each getting a thirty second chance to fight us off in a non-scripted simulation. The padding makes it nearly impossible for us to move with any real speed or accuracy, but the women get the chance to practice their moves and beat us up without doing any real damage.

Mira stands at the very back of the line and after several minutes, I am winded and sweaty. When she gets to the head of the line, determination settles fiercely on her face. Sonya yells *attack* and we run at each other, Mira much faster without the cumbersome outfit. She punches and kicks how she was shown while I try to grab her and pin her down. She kicks out my knees, forcing them to the mat before knocking me face down. I groan when she lands a kick to my ribs that I know I will feel tomorrow, even with the padding.

Pushing myself up to my feet, our eyes meet, hers burning with rage. Sonya calls the women back to the center, but Mira lingers for a moment, still glaring at me as I stay frozen in place. She breaks eye contact to join the group, and I turn to watch her walk away, the ache inside me pressing out and almost cracking my sternum. Derek stumbles over, taking off his head gear.

"They were brutal tonight," he says, breathing heavily. His hair sticks out in all directions and his flushed face has lines from where the straps pressed against his skin. I nod, starting to take off my own gear.

By the time I get it all off, the women have dispersed, some chatting with Sonya and gathering their bags while others walk out toward the main floor. I search for Mira, coming up empty and quickly head out the door. She walks, already halfway to the exit by the time I see her, and I jog over, placing my hand on her shoulder when I catch up.

She whirls around, my hand flying off and deflecting the hit she aims at me. We pause, Mira taking a step back once she sees my face.

"Sorry, probably shouldn't have snuck up on you right after you took a self-defense course," I say. She stares up at me, eyes hard and I swallow.

"What do you want, Harley?" she asks after a moment.

I glance around to take a break from the intensity of her stare. She leans to one side, crossing her arms and tapping her toe. "You did good in there," I offer. She just shrugs and I sigh. "Why did you sign up for the class?"

"I didn't know you worked here," she starts with frost coating the words.

"I figured." The flash of surprise on her face when she noticed me invades my brain. "I meant; most women have a reason for wanting to learn self-defense. Did you see the flyer or something?"

She fidgets and my heart breaks. I want her to say yes, that she just saw an ad for the class on campus and thought it would be fun on a Friday night.

"Just wanted to learn," she whispers, not looking me in

the eye. A few people work out around the gym, and some are still leaving the class. Cheryl speaks to a few women at the front desk, probably trying to convince them to sign up for a membership.

I pull Mira off the walking path and closer to the wall so that people can't overhear us. "What happened?"

She meets my eyes and opens her mouth, but I cut her off.

"I know something happened."

Her mouth snaps shut and screws into a scowl. We stare at each other for a beat before she glances at my hand still gripping her upper arm. I let go instantly and Mira leans into the wall beside us.

"I think I got followed back to West Tower after the party the other night." She speaks at the ground while she says it and I flex my hand to stop myself from touching her again.

Anger blazes back to life behind my ribs. "You think?" My voice sounds much calmer than I thought it would.

She nods. "I heard footsteps behind me and saw someone, so I ran for it. Made it inside but then I didn't see anyone there." She plays with her fingers before suddenly looking back up at me, panic stricken. "You can't tell Ramsey about this."

I frown. "Why not?" Relaxing my fists, I realize my nails bit into my palms when she told me what happened.

"He'll freak and probably glue himself to my side. I don't want to worry him." Her finger points at me as she stands at full height below my chin. "Promise me you won't say anything."

The ferocity is back in her eyes, fire burning through her words. I nod before realizing it. "I won't say anything." She deflates in relief. "But one class isn't enough. You'll need to keep practicing the moves to make them muscle memory."

She nods but frowns. "Okay, I'll practice. Can I go now?"

I raise an eyebrow at her. "Come on, Mira. You hate exercise. I know you're not going to practice the moves on your own."

She puts her hands on her hips. "Are you trying to get me to sign up for a membership right now?"

I take a step back, unsure how we got here. I want Mira to be safe but can't exactly avoid her if she comes to the gym regularly. "No, I'm just saying you'll need someone to run through the scenarios with."

Mira's eyes flash and she drops her arms, glancing around. Her eyes find the corkboard on the nearby wall. She walks over and pulls one of the quick-rip tickets off the bottom of a burgundy flyer for personal training. "Fine, I'll get a trainer to run through them with me. Happy?"

I smirk. "That's for *my* open slot."

She crushes the slip in her hand, fist shaking as her face flames.

A hand claps my back and Derek appears beside me. "Boss-man trying to get you to sign up for training?"

Mira leans over and drops the slip into a nearby trash. "Nope, quite the opposite actually."

"Oh." Derek's hand falls off my back. "Well, if you want more defense training, I can always help you practice." He winks and I tamp down the urge to punch him.

The need intensifies when Mira turns her full attention on him and *smiles*. "Actually, that would be perfect. Harley was just saying that I need to keep up with the moves to get them to really stick."

"Your slots are booked up, Derek," I say after forcibly releasing my jaw.

Derek waves nonchalantly, not even looking my way. "I

can make extra room in my schedule for such a beautiful client.”

Mira beams and my shoulders tense.

“Well, I actually have an opening, so if anyone is going to train Mira, it’s going to be me.” I cut in between them and grab her arm. “If you’ll excuse us, Derek, I have to get her back to campus. Be back in a bit.”

Mira opens her mouth, but only a squeak escapes as I pull her out of my gym.

9

Harley doesn't release me until we stand in front of his truck in the parking lot. My flesh tingles from where he held it and it makes me that much more upset that I still react to him when mad. "I literally just learned a move to break out of that exact hold," I bite out.

"Then why didn't you use it?" He folds his arms over his chest and the move makes his uncovered arm muscles flex.

"Didn't think I'd ever have to use it on you for real." His face falls for a moment before he hides the reaction, replacing it with hostility.

"This is why you need to practice the moves from tonight. It should be reflex to break out of that hold."

"Yeah, okay I get it. I'll practice the moves."

"I wasn't joking about training you. You're taking my open training slot."

I gape at him. "You can't be serious, Harley. You've avoided being in the same room as me for years and now you want to be my personal trainer?"

He flinches at the start of my question. "You need

someone to hold you accountable. I've got the time available." He shrugs.

I look around the dark parking lot as if someone will come up and somehow make sense of what is happening. Harley wants to train me. Harley wants to spend time with me. The image of him and the girl on the bed flashes in my head for the millionth time and my heart squeezes.

"You don't have to do this, Harley. Thanks for the offer, but I don't think it's a good idea."

"Why not?" He drops his arms to his sides.

Why is he pushing this so hard?

I shrug, glancing down at my feet. I didn't think I would ever have to justify needing to avoid each other to him.

"Mira, look at me."

I hesitate before turning toward him. The hostility has ebbed, and his eyes bore into mine.

"I want you to feel safe on your own. It'll just be a few weeks to make sure you have the moves ingrained." He closes his mouth and I sense he wants to say something more. Instead, he stares down at me for a moment before adding, "Besides, Ramsey would kill me if something happened to you because I didn't teach you how to defend yourself."

I roll my eyes, my stomach twisting as I break his intense stare. "Fine. I'll train with you."

He nods, studying me for a second before tilting his head toward the truck.

"I can just walk back, it's fine."

He sighs. "What did I just say? I would never hear the end of it if your brother found out I let you walk home in the dark." He walks over and opens the passenger door, gesturing for me to get in. I take a deep breath and hop into the cab of his truck.

My nerves skyrocket after he shuts the door. *What the fuck is going on?* Harley is going to train me. Harley is going to drive me back to campus.

He opens the driver's side door a few seconds later and gets behind the wheel. I click my seatbelt on, and he pulls out of the parking lot.

"I'm in West Tower," I say.

"I know," he replies, turning left at a light. "Did you walk all the way to the gym tonight?"

"No, I took the campus bus." I relax a little in the seat and stare out the window to keep from watching him. "Nearly missed it after I dropped my bag off at Bentley's."

"Why did you drop your stuff off at Marshall's?" His one-handed grip on the steering wheel tightens.

"I'm staying with him for a couple days. My roommate's boyfriend visits on the weekends." I shrug. Harley's face screws up and he glances over at me.

"You could always stay in one of the guest rooms at the house." His words seem benign, but his tone is annoyed. He takes another turn, entering campus from the opposite side of West Tower and cutting through the center toward it.

"I'm fine with Bentley. Wouldn't want to put you out with my presence." I throw some bite into the words, remembering my anger toward him. He pulls off into the parking lot of the English building. "What are you doing?" He starts to head back toward the road.

"Taking you to the house. You can stay with us for the weekend." He turns on his blinker as a group of students crosses leisurely in front of the parking lot's exit.

"Like hell I will." I unbuckle my seatbelt and open the door, hopping out. I start to walk toward West Tower, hearing Harley's car door open and close as his footsteps get closer.

"Mira! Get back in the car," he calls.

I hasten my pace, making it beyond the parking lot, but he easily catches up to me. I whip around when I hear him on my heels, and he startles back at my advance. "Why are you even talking to me, Harley? You have no right to dictate any part of my life, especially after ignoring me for the last few years. So, why the sudden interest in where I spend my weekend? I know you don't really care about me since you've been nothing but an ass before tonight."

"I have not." His voice shakes as he tries to deny it.

"No, you're right. You've been perfectly polite at every instance. Just short of cold, really." He flinches, but the rage pouring out of me couldn't care less. "And all because of that stupid kiss two years ago, right?" He looks away and I shake my head. "It was a dumb high school crush, Harley. Get over it. I already did." The words burn my throat, but I force my voice to stay even and hold my head high.

His grey eyes whip up to mine. "Yeah right," he snaps and steps toward me. I back up the same amount. "You never got over your 'dumb high school crush,' Mira," he says, holding up his hands to make air quotes. "I've seen you watch me when you thought I wouldn't notice." He keeps advancing on me with each word and I continue to step back, throat tightening. "I've seen the spark in your eyes when I look at you, know that smile you have when I say something to you. You never got over it, and you can't lie to me and say you did."

"I'm not ly—

Brick bites into my back through my tee shirt as Harley pushes me up against the building and slams his mouth over mine. Shock freezes me in place as his hands come up to cup and angle my face. His tongue slides across my bottom lip, and I gasp; Harley taking that as an open invitation to deepen the kiss. I kiss him back with just as much fervor, hands coming up to dig my nails into the sleeves of his shirt. His hands slide down my neck and shoulders before finding purchase on my waist. He bunches my shirt a bit as his hips press into mine, pinning me further into the wall. I can feel him hard against my stomach and shiver. He releases my waist, sliding his hands to the back of my thighs and gripping them as he lifts me. I wrap my legs around his waist and throw my arms around his neck to bring him even closer. The position aligns the apex of my thighs with his erection, and I moan into his mouth.

The sound seems to freeze Harley beneath me. He pulls his head back, searching my face before muttering, "Shit."

I hit the ground in the next moment, pain radiating up my tailbone. My palms land down in the dirt, trying to catch my fall and I groan. I wipe my hands together and look up as Harley backs away from me, horror struck. "That was a mistake," he whispers. His pace quickens before he turns and jogs back to his truck.

"Clearly," I say to myself, heart sinking as I watch him pull out of the lot and drive away.

10

I walk back to West Tower, replaying the kiss in my head. Reaching Bentley's door, I knock, and tears instantly appear when he pulls it open, smiling. The smile falls immediately, and he pulls me inside. Setting me on the couch, he wraps a giant pillowy comforter around my body.

"What happened?"

I recap the entire night for Bentley, starting with the self-defense course being held at the gym where Harley works. Bentley's eyes widen to the point that I think he might hurt himself when I tell him Harley kissed me. Practically consumed me is more like it, but I spare that detail. Then I get to the part about him dropping me on the ground and Bentley jumps up. I scramble to block him from leaving, telling him he is not about to go start a fight with Harley at the Ravens' mansion.

"Why the hell not?" he asks.

I have my hands up against his chest in a weak attempt to hold him back. "Because Ramsey cannot find out about this." Bentley searches my eyes as I use them to plead my case.

"Fine," he finally says. "But next time I see Harley, I'm at least going to punch him."

I sigh as he sits back down on the couch, arms crossing. Taking a few deep breaths, I join him. We silently start playing Mario Kart and after beating me a few times, Bentley seems cooled down, but I keep getting distracted, my brain spiraling over everything.

After his sixth consecutive win, he declares this boring and calls Autumn to come over with Aria. I spend the entirety of the movie we watch thinking about Harley and slowly getting mad. The anger swirls in my gut and I have a death grip on my soda to stop my hand from shaking. He finally kissed me back. Then he had to go and ruin it like an asshole. And I don't even know when I'll get the chance to tell him off because he'll probably go back to his running away routine like he did when I kissed him.

Autumn and Aria leave around two and Bentley yawns, saying he needs to go pass out. He hugs me quick and disappears into his room.

I lay on the couch in the dark and the anger slowly dissipates into a heart squelching pain in my chest and throat. Harley finally kissed me back. *He* kissed me. And yet I still feel like I somehow did something wrong yet again. My eyes burn but I refuse to cry this time.

What the fuck were the last two years about? I thought he avoided me because he was disgusted that I kissed him, or thought I was some stupid kid obsessed with him. But if that was the case, he wouldn't have kissed me tonight. He wouldn't have offered to train me, offered to drive me home, gotten mad that I was staying with Bentley.

I turn onto my side, tucking my hands under Bentley's

pillow. The clock on the entertainment center says 3:26. I stare at it until 4:12. Tears slide unbidden down my face, trailing over the bridge of my nose. I feel so confused and for some reason want to seek comfort from the same person who caused this pain. I close my eyes and slowly lose consciousness, the look of horror on Harley's face swimming in my mind.

Pounding on the door wakes me not even two hours later. I sit up and grip my head as the world dips for a second. My mouth is dry, and my under-eyes feel puffy. I know a shower and a few glasses of water will make a world of difference, but the pounding sounds again, and I groan when it echoes inside my skull.

I flip the comforter off and cross the room. Ripping the door open, I groan, "What?" then inhale sharply.

Harley stands before me; fist raised to pound more. His eyes flick over me, before jerking his chin over his shoulder. "Training starts now. Let's go."

I glance around, not sure what exactly could convince me this is real right now. Accepting I don't know how to wake up from this dream, I go to shut the door, but Harley's hand flies out and stops it from moving more than an inch.

"Are you fucking insane? What makes you think I'll still train with you after you quite literally *dropped* me on the ground last night?" I walk away, heading to the kitchen and turning on Bentley's coffee maker. Harley follows, the door closing behind him.

"I shouldn't have left you there," he says monotonously.

I scoff. "No fucking shit." I turn away to get a mug from the dishwasher, hands shaking with rage again. "Go home, Harley. I don't want to do this anymore."

A door opens behind Harley and Bentley emerges, eyes

half closed and hand scratching the back of his head. "What was all that noise?"

"Harley's here," I say.

Bentley's eyes pop open completely and his face clouds with murderous thunder. He walks out of his room and right up to Harley. They are almost matched in height, Bentley only falling short by an inch or two.

"Get the fuck out," Bentley hisses.

"Not without Mira," Harley steps forward, their chests touching. I set my mug down quickly and wedge myself between them, facing Bentley.

"It's okay, Bent." I pat his chest. "Go back to bed. I can get rid of him." Bentley doesn't break eye contact with Harley for longer than I want, but finally his eyes slide down to me.

"Holler if you need me to throw him out." He glares back at Harley before smirking and quickly pecking my cheek, then turning on his heel.

I wait for the door to close before turning around and poking Harley. "Do not threaten Bentley," I hiss. Harley raises a surprised brow, and I lower my finger and walk back around him to get my mug from the counter.

"No coffee before our run," Harley says.

I let out a sharp laugh. "I'm not running with you, Harley."

He steps forward, taking the mug from my hands and putting it back on the counter. He then walks to the fridge and opens the door. Emerging a moment later with a water bottle, he tosses it to me. "You need to hydrate before we leave."

I slam the bottle down on the counter. "*We* are not leaving. *You* are leaving and I don't care what you do once you're gone."

He leans back against the fridge and crosses his arms. I turn to leave the kitchen.

His voice comes out low as he says, "I'll tell Ramsey someone followed you home from the party."

I stop dead, whirling back around.

He nods toward the open bathroom door. "Go get changed."

I study him. "You're bluffing."

He shrugs. "Try me."

I keep searching his eyes. He holds steady, giving nothing away. "Why are you doing this?" I ask, my voice breaking.

He shifts on his feet but doesn't look away. "Go get changed."

I grit my teeth and take a deep breath through my nose. Stalking over to the couch, I unzip the duffel bag beside my makeshift bed. Harley walks in from the kitchen, eyeing my setup. Relief softens his features until I pull out the clothes I wore to the class last night.

"You don't have anything else?"

I search for a clean pair of underwear and socks in the shadows of my bag. "Didn't really pack with the intention of doing another workout," I bite out. My hands still shake with rage as I dig around. I feel lightheaded from it and hope the run will at least shake some of this, though I doubt it will be far away with the object of my ire running beside me.

"Let's just go to your room and get some fresh clothes."

I snap my head up, narrowing my eyes at him. Harley stands rigidly, hands fisted at his sides, eyes locked on the leggings in my hand.

I smirk. "I think these will do for today." I pull out a pair of underwear and socks and head into the bathroom to change.

I hear Harley mutter, "Fucking hell," under his breath before I shut the door. His torture fractionally eases my anger.

I emerge minutes later, after splashing cold water on my face to make it look less puffy. Harley silently walks out, and I write a note on the whiteboard outside of Bentley's room, telling him I will be back in a little while, before following Harley out of the suite. Harley stands holding the elevator door open, waiting for me. We step into the elevator, facing forward with as much distance between us as we can get.

Once outside, Harley shows me a few stretches to do before every run. I bite back commentary about this being the only time I will run, not wanting to let on that I am actively trying to find a way out of this.

"We need to work on your stamina. I'll go through the defense moves with you and show you a few more, but the first thing you need to get good at doing is running. The next option should be shouting for help if you're ever in a dangerous situation."

I roll my eyes along with my shoulders.

"I'm serious, Mira. Fighting should be a last resort, not your go to response."

"Yeah, yeah, run, scream, then fight. I got it." I bend down to touch my toes.

"Take this seriously," Harley says when I right myself. His jaw has to unclench to spit the words out.

"Let's just go, okay?"

He points down the sidewalk and I take off at a light jog.

We jog in complete silence. Well, not complete silence. The sound of my breathing bangs around in my ears as I start to severely lack oxygen. My lungs drag in sharply, the feeling icy in my chest. I wheeze out, stuttering as I try to maintain pace. Harley matches my stride, keeping up effortlessly. We run on the sidewalk of Ring Road, arcing around campus. I decide I need to make it at least halfway today and nearly cry when I see the admin building that serves as the marker I made up in my head. Collapsing onto the grass in front of it, I throw my arms out wide while my chest rises and caves rapidly.

"Get up," Harley says, toeing my sneaker with his foot.

I pointedly do not answer. The fact that I made it this far is frankly a miracle. I stare up at the early morning haze, trying to feel anything but the thrum pulsing through my body.

"Come on, Mira, we're only halfway, you can't stop now."

"You should just leave me here," I huff out. My eyes slide up to his. "We both already know you're proficient at leaving me on the ground."

Harley closes his eyes and pinches the bridge of his nose before dropping down to sit beside me. He pulls more water bottles out of his pockets, placing one in my hand before uncapping his own and sipping it. His other arm hangs loosely around his knees as he casually watches the campus slowly wake up around us. He doesn't even pant or take a couple deep breaths, like a dick.

I sit up after a few minutes, opening the water bottle and chugging a few gulps. Harley's hand shoots out and pulls the bottle from my lips. "Slowly," he says. "You'll get cramps if you down it."

"Why are you doing this? Why not just go back to hating me from a distance?" I take a small sip this time. The water slides down my throat, easing the dry burn that formed when we ran.

"Doesn't matter how I feel. I told you last night, Ramsey

would kill me if he found out I left you defenseless." Harley squints as he says it, seeming fascinated with the building across the street. I shake my head.

"So, we're not going to discuss last night?"

His eye twitches. "Nope." He sips his water.

I shake my head, glancing away from him and pulling up some grass as my breathing slowly returns to normal. When I've sipped half the bottle of water and don't choke on air, Harley stands, holding his hand out. I push myself off the ground, placing my water bottle in his hand once I stand. He gives me an unimpressed look before jerking his head back toward West Tower.

"We can walk the rest for today." We set off and I watch the light edge across the world as we round the rest of campus. Not a single word passes between us, and I pretend Harley isn't even there. The morning around us is peaceful and I find my anger from earlier easing despite my company. By the time we stand in front of West Tower, I almost forget to stop, starting to head in when Harley clears his throat.

I turn back from the doorway.

"I'll pick you up tomorrow morning. We can head to the gym before opening and practice the stuff you learned last night." He turns to leave, and I do the same before hearing him call, "And you better be in *your* dorm room when I show up."

11

Harley

"Do the stretches I showed you yesterday," I bite out, taking a breath to try to quell the brewing storm in my gut. Mira frowns at my tone and the image of her looking up at me dumbstruck from the ground flashes before my eyes. A barb of guilt cuts through the anger and lust swirling inside me, and I start doing my own stretches to stop myself from saying anything else.

I pull my arm across my chest, stretching my shoulders, when Mira bends down to stretch her hamstrings. She touches her toes, but my eyes get stuck on her ass, images of walking over and grabbing her hips playing in my mind. I turn away quickly, finishing my warmup.

The night I fucked up and kissed Mira is etched into my brain and plays on a loop constantly. The whole drive home, I beat myself up each time I remembered the feeling of her against me. Her moan echoed in my ears and my dick jerked as more blood left my brain and tried to convince me to turn around. Anger clouded my judgement and I saw red when she said she got over me. Just thinking of her eyes rolling as she called it a "dumb high school crush" makes my teeth gnash together. I always convinced myself that staying away from her was the best course of action, figuring I would eventually stop noticing her in rooms full of people, but the idea of Mira getting over me burned in my throat.

I paced my room for hours that night trying to figure out what to do next. I needed to stay away from her, even more now that I had been the one to initiate. There was no way Mira would just let this go if I was around her one on one. I would have to get someone else to train her. Maybe I could trade with Sonya or Grace for one of their clients. The memory of Derek flirting with Mira brought my earlier anger back to the surface. I stopped in the center of my room and groaned, rubbing my hands over my face. I couldn't give up training Mira.

And now that I stand with her back in the training room an hour before the gym opens, I question that decision for the millionth time.

She was only half awake when I showed up outside her dorm this morning, rubbing her eyes and yawning. I smiled at how adorable she looked, quickly hiding it and glad that she missed my slip because she turned to grab a bag before shutting the door to her suite.

We didn't say anything as I drove, tension building in my shoulders once we were in the small, enclosed space. I had to fight the urge to drag her to the storage room or into my office when we walked into the gym. She thankfully dressed in a different set of leggings and tee shirt than the last two days. If I had to watch her move in the textured pair she wore the night I kissed her, stopping myself from a repeat performance might have been impossible. I already spent a decent percentage of time during the jog yesterday rubbing my palms against my thighs, trying to alleviate the itch to reach out and touch her again.

"So, what are we doing today, boss?"

I turn around and raise a questioning eyebrow at the epithet.

She shrugs. "You've been bossy lately."

I frown at her assessment. I don't want her to feel forced to be here. "Mira, do you want me to train you?"

She stares up at me with a crinkled brow. "You blackmail me into going for a run with you, make me get up at the asscrack of dawn and come all the way down here, do my warmup stretches, and now you're checking to see if I actually want to be here?" I wait, flinching a little when she mentions the blackmail. "Too late, dude, I'm already here. Let's get on with it." She waves her hands in front of me impatiently.

I sigh and glance at the ceiling for a second. "Whatever. Let's run the combo they did at the end of class the other night. I can assess which moves need improvement and how much you remember." We stand opposite each other already, so I reach out and start the fight scenario from Friday night. Mira counters and we keep running the moves repeatedly.

When we've been at it for over a half hour, I call for her to stop, and Mira stands up fully, panting. "Need a break?" I ask and she nods. I walk over to the side and grab us each a bottle of water, tossing one to her which she catches before sitting down on the mat. I stay on the side of the room, sipping the water and watching her. She sips hers this time instead of guzzling it and I smile slightly.

"Why did you come back to our house so late last weekend?" She stares down at the floor, not bothering to look up when she asks.

I fidget with the cap of my bottle, ignoring the pull to think back on the dinner at my parents'.

"You said you got kicked out again." She looks up this time, meeting my gaze. "What did you mean?"

I watch her as she waits for me to answer. "Why are you asking?"

She shrugs, eyes falling back down. "That was the first time you spoke to me when we were alone, and I didn't really understand what you meant." I sigh. "We're not talking about the other night, so I thought it'd be safer to talk about that one."

I glance away from her, pushing down images of Friday night. If I get hard right now, she will definitely be able to tell in my loose gym shorts.

"I got into another fight with my parents," I say, figuring her logic of sticking to a safer topic might help. I look back to find her staring up at me with a confused expression. "They kicked me out when I dropped out of the Coast. Cut me off entirely. So, when they couldn't force me to act the way they wanted that night, they kicked me out again. I was supposed to stay with them for the weekend, so I just walked over to your house, figuring April wouldn't mind."

She nods and takes another sip. "I didn't know they cut you off entirely. I just figured the conversation didn't go well when you told them, based off what Ramsey said."

I lean back against the wall. "What did Ramsey tell you?"

"Just that you dropped out. That college wasn't really for you and that your parents didn't take it well." Mira peers at me, a bit sheepish, probably because she just revealed that she asked about me. I keep myself from smiling. I knew Mira didn't get over me like she tried to make it seem.

"They want me to become a politician; are really set on

it, to be honest." I stare down at the cap in my hand, flipping it between my fingers. "I didn't like any of my classes and spent most of my time at the campus gym when I wasn't with the guys. I wanted to switch over to business, liking the idea of owning my own gym, but when I brought it up to my parents, they flipped. They had this whole idea of me becoming some public figure and I couldn't get them to understand that isn't me." I look up at her, seeing her heartbreak for me on full display. The expression makes me breathless for a moment before I shake my head and look away. "They cut me off financially and I didn't have access to any of my savings, so I dropped out since I couldn't exactly afford tuition."

"Is that when you got the job here?" Mira smiles at me when I look back, hope and pride swirling in her eyes. I bask for a second in the idea that she is proud of me before telling her the truth.

"Mira, I own this gym." Her face falls back into confusion and a bit of astonishment, and I can't hold back the short laugh that escapes. "I went to your mom after my parents kicked me out, just wanting to see if I could stay with you guys while I figured out what to do next. She made me explain everything that happened and when I was done, she asked if I thought I really needed a business degree. I told her I had already dropped out and couldn't afford tuition, but she told me if I wanted to go back to school, she would pay the tuition, but to her it sounded like my major wasn't the issue. It was that I had a goal and was putting it off because I thought I had to." I pause, remembering my shock when April offered to pay for me to go back to school.

"Sounds like some wise shit my mom would say." Mira scoots closer, eagerly waiting for the rest of the story.

I snort. "Yeah, well she then offered to help me get a small business loan and open up my own gym." I gesture around me. "She helped me scout out locations back home and here, then cosigned the loan when we settled on this place."

Mira's jaw drops. "Mom helped you start your own business?"

I nod and her face lights up.

"You run this place?"

"It's been mine for a little over two years."

She glances around, looking out at the main floor through the open doorway, as if seeing it for the first time.

"The campus gym is small and has outdated machines. Plus, there are no training rooms or classes offered. So, I figured being right by the campus would bring in new clientele every year and fill in the need for more fitness options. Plus, I can still live with the guys for now and get the college experience without suffering through classes I didn't want to go to. Your dad even helped me in the first year to learn all the administrative stuff that goes into running this place, like payroll and taxes and shit."

Her eyes come back to me, and the pride is back in full force. "This is amazing, Harley. I had no idea they helped you out so much."

I shrug before rubbing the back of my neck. That is probably my fault with the whole avoiding her plan. Kind of left her off the list of people I talk to about my life after that night. She looks down at her water bottle, putting the cap back on as heat creeps into her face. I bite back the urge to ask what she is thinking, instead asking, "How are you liking school so far?"

She shrugs, not looking up.

"Come on, Mira. You're not loving your art classes?"

Her head whips up. "How'd you know I'm taking art classes?"

I glance away. "Ramsey mentioned it." I uncap my water bottle. "Plus you were always painting and sketching so I always thought you'd go to school for it."

She brings her knees up to her chest and hugs them. "I'm working on a minor in drawing. My major is chemistry."

I nearly spit out a mouthful of water. Swallowing it thickly, I release a laugh once my throat is clear. "Why? You hate science."

"I do not!" she cries, but her voice lilts at the end. I give her a *be real* look. "It's not my favorite, but Dad thought it would be smarter. There's a lot of opportunity for women in STEM right now and I'll make better money in the long run." She puts her chin on her knees, staring out at nothing.

I watch her for a minute, getting lost a bit myself. "You should go to school for what you want to do," I whisper, and her eyes meet mine. "Who cares about the money? You love art. You shouldn't have to suffer through science classes just to hopefully one day have more job security."

Her eyes harden. "Back off, Harley. You don't get to tell me what I should do after basically trying to disappear from my life for years. You don't get to act like you know me."

Her reaction awakens the anger that had been quiet this morning, and I push off the wall, standing at my full height over her. "I grew up with you, Mira. I sure as hell know you. You were practically my sister. And you're doing that thing you always do where you suffer to try to make your parents happy. Being a martyr for them is always going to bite you in the ass."

She lets go of her knees and pushes herself off the floor.

"Your sister?" she screeches. "Sure didn't seem like you thought of me as your sister the other night with your tongue in my mouth."

I bristle, taking a step toward her. "You're Ramsey's little sister. Ramsey is my brother; therefore, I *have to* think of you as my little sister."

"Says who?" she screams, looking around. "Is that why you avoided me for so long? Because I ruined your stupid image of joining my perfect little family?" Her voice turns mocking at the end.

I growl. "Stop pressing the issue. You can't get everything you want. And I don't want you like that." My chest squeezes as the lie slips out. Shock spreads over Mira's face, and she stumbles back a few steps.

Knocking sounds on the open door to the room and I look over to see Derek popping his head in. "Everything okay in here?"

I glance at the clock, realizing we open in five minutes. "Yeah. Fine. Just finishing up."

Derek nods before smiling at Mira and walking away. Mira walks over to her bag, throwing her bottle into it and roughly zipping it up, never looking in my direction.

I roll my neck and close my eyes for a second, counting to ten. "Do you need a ride back to campus?"

"No," she says, looking up to meet my eyes. "Bentley is coming to pick me up."

Red clouds my vision, and I bite out, "Good," before storming out of the room. I head straight past Cheryl and Derek at the front desk and slam the door to my office. The urge to punch something swells, but my fist already took plenty of damage the last few weeks, so I open one of my desk drawers and pull out the hand wraps I keep here.

They're scarlet, not only matching my simmering rage, but wholly reminding me of the girl who created it.

Twenty minutes in and I am already coated in sweat. My employees avoided me when I came out, hands taped up and steam practically coming out of my nose like a bull. A tap on my shoulder is the only thing that stops me from continuing to pummel a leather punching bag in the corner of the gym.

Ramsey stands behind me, holding his hands up when I whirl around. "Sorry, didn't realize how in the zone you were. Working something out?" I glance around, realizing the gym has started to fill up with the early morning rush. I hadn't noticed anything after leaving Mira.

"Saw Marshall pulling into the parking lot when I got here. He get a membership?"

I sigh, starting to unwrap my fingers. "Maybe. Cheryl handles most of the sign ups now so he might have been brought in by her."

Ramsey grins. "She still throwing her chest in your face?"

I roll my eyes.

"Don't see why you don't take the offer." He looks across the room at the front desk where Cheryl greets some people.

I turn away. "I'm not going to sleep with my employee, Rams."

He turns back toward me with his brows raised. "I figured you'd sleep with anything that walks, considering that's been the policy since we got here." Ramsey tends to keep girls around for longer than I do. But I couldn't exactly tell him I started comparing most women to his sister.

"Employees are off limits." I lean against the side of a nearby machine. "Besides, I like a bit more chase."

Ramsey scoffs. "Since when?"

"Don't you have a workout to go do?" I point to the treadmills quickly filling up. He laughs, giving me a mock salute before heading over to them. I shake my head, finish unwrapping my hands, and head back to my office. I put away the wraps and sit down at my desk, logging onto my computer to do some actual work.

"Bentley, stop."

My head lifts when I hear Mira's raw voice. The door to my office is open and I can see Bentley with his hands on the front desk, Cheryl standing in front of him. Mira stands at his side, eyes red rimmed and face blotchy, pulling on his arm.

Marshall twists it out of her grip, looking past Cheryl and meeting my eyes. I stand and walk out of my office, holding his angry gaze. "Something the matter?"

"What did you do to her to make her this upset?" Bentley bites out. Cheryl looks down at Mira who grabs Bentley's arm again and pulls, purposely avoiding her gaze. He lets her this time but stands his ground. "You need to stop being a dick and leave Mira alone." His voice gets louder as he issues the order.

"Bentley, stop," Mira pleads, glancing around the gym as a few people look over at the commotion. I cross my arms, holding myself together while my chest cracks at the sight of Mira so distressed.

"I don't care what you have on her, deal's off," Bentley continues, pointing his finger across the desk at me. "Stay. Away."

Ramsey walks up. "What's going on?"

"Nothing," I say in a calm voice and at the same time as Mira says it in a panic. Ramsey looks between the two of us, then over at Bentley who still glares at me.

"We were just leaving," Mira says, tugging on Bentley,

who lets her move him a few steps back. He glances down, seeing how flustered she is and sighs.

He turns to Ramsey and says, "It's nothing, man. I'll see you around," before putting his arm around Mira's shoulders and walking out with her. I watch them get into his car through the glass doors, biting the inside of my cheek so hard I taste blood.

12

"Why the hell would you do that?" I yell when Bentley pulls out of the gym parking lot.

He grips the steering wheel with two hands, knuckles white. "He's made you cry twice in the last three days, Mir! He blackmailed you using your brother. You should have told Ramsey what's going on. He shouldn't be friends with that asshole."

I throw my head back against the headrest. "I'm not telling Ramsey anything." Turning to look at my best friend, I point my finger at him. "And neither will you." Bentley scowls at the windshield, turning into campus. We pass the building Harley pushed me up against and my heart squeezes as his words from the gym filter through my mind. *You can't get everything you want. And I don't want you like that.* I feel the nail in the coffin scratching against my ribcage. "I mean it, Bent. Leave it alone. It's done. You didn't need to go in there and do that."

Bentley looks over at me quickly. "Why are you protecting him, Mir?"

We pull into the West Tower lot. "Ramsey is Harley's

best friend. Harley's parents kicked him out and disowned him. The guys are all he has right now. I would never do anything to take that away from him." Ramsey noticed Harley being curt with me over the years, not hanging out so much when I was around. When he asked me about what happened, I could have told him, but I covered for Harley. There was no need to ruin their friendship just because he didn't reciprocate my feelings.

Bentley parks the car, turning to face me in his seat. "Mira, he used Ramsey against you. He ignored you for three years and is now playing games with you. He doesn't deserve your protection, and Ramsey deserves a better friend."

"Harley has never been a bad friend to Ramsey." I look out the windshield to avoid Bentley's eyes. "Doesn't matter what he does to me; I won't take that away from either of them."

Bentley puts his head against the steering wheel and groans. "Fine, I won't say anything to Ramsey." I relax into the seat. "But you need to keep your distance from Harley. He's playing games with you."

"You don't need to worry about that." I get out of the car and Bentley follows. "Harley's not going to be training me anymore."

Bentley seems satisfied with that as we walk into the dorm.

He also seems particularly happy when I report that I haven't seen Harley all week when I show up at his dorm the next Friday with my duffel bag, ready to camp out for the weekend. Christopher showed up while I was in class and was sitting on my couch playing some video game on the TV in my suite while Janette laid on the other one reading. I immediately grabbed my pre-packed bag and told her I was staying with Bentley for the weekend. I heard Christopher murmur, "Good," under his breath, but Janette at least took a moment to chastise him.

"That's good, Mir. You're better off. Fuck him." He rolls the sleeves of his dress shirt up to his elbows.

"Why are you so dressed up?" I pull a bag of popcorn out of his cabinet and throw it in the microwave.

He drops his arms. "Oh shit, I thought I told you. Cassie said yes when I asked her out yesterday. We're going to that hibachi place in town."

I fold my arms over my chest and lean against the counter. "That's great!" I try not to frown. "I guess I'll take this to my room since Autumn and Aria are at that sorority initiation thing tonight." I turn toward the microwave, watching the numbers count down.

"You can stay here if you want. I'll be back at some point and Axel's out again doing God knows what."

I nod. "Thanks. Anything's better than sitting in my room quietly while Janette and Christopher argue in the living room."

Bentley walks over and hugs me. With an extra squeeze, he leans back, hands still on my shoulders. "You going to be okay on your own here for a bit?"

I nod emphatically and slap a smile on my face. "You mean here alone with your giant TV, endless streaming services, and hours of time to binge watch the teen dramas you won't watch with me anymore?"

"As long as there's no vampires or fairies, I'll watch it. I don't think those are difficult parameters."

I laugh and push him away. "Go pick up Cassie."

"Aw, don't be like that." He throws an arm around my shoulder. "I got time for a round of Mario Kart, if you want?"

The microwave dings and I turn and pull the steaming

bag out by the edges. I reach up and grab a big bowl. "Nah, with my luck, you'll win and then leave, and I won't be able to get the TV to the right HDMI input." I rip open the bag and dump the popcorn into the bowl.

Bentley pecks my cheek, and I push his face away, missing him nabbing a handful of my popcorn. "Hey!" I yell as he shoves it in his mouth. I jump to try to grab his hand. He smiles widely, popcorn falling out his mouth, before dancing away from my flailing kick and laughing.

"Have fun!" I yell while he snags his jacket off the back of the couch and waves before leaving.

The moment the door closes behind him, silence settles in and my face falls. I munch on popcorn as I plop onto the couch and flick through the endless options on all the different TV apps. I can't settle on anything, ache sitting inside my chest. I hear a group of people pass by the door, laughing as they get onto the elevator and the ache grows. I mostly spent my week going to my classes and then in my room when I was free. Autumn and Aria had been invited to check out a sorority after going to the activities fair that I had to miss for one of my chem labs. Bentley and Axel started hanging out, meeting up for lunch and playing video games when I came over to lounge on the couch, feeling weirdly like a third wheel to them. Now here I am, alone in their suite, while everyone I know goes out and lives their lives.

For a moment, I wonder what Harley is doing tonight.

You can't get everything you want. And I don't want you like that.

The image of the girl and him on his bed hits and I flinch, dropping the remote. The ache expands tenfold.

I set the half empty bowl of popcorn down and grab my

phone. It rings twice before Ramsey's voice filters through the speaker. "What's up?"

"Hey, nothing, just realizing I didn't see you at all this week. How are things?" I bite my lip.

Ramsey says something muffled away from the phone. "Things are good. Are you okay? You sound down."

I nod, knowing he can't see me. "Yeah, I'm fine. Just wanted to see what you're doing tonight?"

"I've got tickets to a show in the city tonight. Going to see that band I showed you over the summer."

My shoulders fall. "That sounds awesome." Harley's face flashes in my mind again. "Who are you going with?"

"I'm taking this girl I met at your party, actually. I'm leaving to go get her in a few."

"Okay, I'll let you go then. Have fun." I pull my phone from my ear, ready to hang up.

"Hey, bug."

I put the phone to my ear again. Tears sting the corners of my eyes, and I fight the urge to sniffle them away. "Yeah?"

"You sure you're okay? I can skip the show if you want to hang out?"

I pull the phone away and swallow down the lump in my throat. "No! Go have a good time. I'm just going to hang here at Bentley's tonight."

"Why are you calling to hang out with me if you're already with Marshall?"

I close my eyes and swear quickly in my head. "He's out on a date tonight. I'm just in his suite right now."

Ramsey's voice comes out more forcefully. "Why aren't you in your suite?"

I sigh. "Because my roommate's the worst, and her boyfriend visits every weekend. I didn't want to just sit in my room while they take over the suite. Go to your show, Rams. I'll be fine."

I hear Ramsey exhale on the other end. "Mir, if you want me to cancel, I will. You don't have to spend the night on your own."

I shake my head. "Go to the show, Ramsey. I'm fine, really."

"Okay. But if you get bored you can always stop by and use the pool or something. You have a key so just let yourself in, none of the guys will care."

"Thanks, Ramsey."

"Love you, bug."

"Love you, too." I hang up and sniff back the emotions welling in my eyes. Picking up the remote, I resign myself to my fate, turning to the cable network and flicking through the channels till I find a gameshow that looks weird and holds my interest. I burrow further into the couch and grab my popcorn again.

The show soon loses its luster, and I start flicking through to see what else is on when the commercials irritate me. I feel antsy and restless. I could work on my art project. I brought my stuff in case I got the urge but doing homework on a Friday night feels lame. Then again, sitting alone in my friend's dorm watching TV also feels lame.

A knock on the door makes me jump and I spill some popcorn. I sigh, putting the bowl on the coffee table and brushing the pieces that fell into my hand. Walking them over to the trash can in the kitchen, I drop them in as another round of knocking hits the door.

"Coming," I yell, running over.

I pull the door open and startle, coming face to face with Harley. He has his hands in his pockets, looking a bit wary. "Hi," he says.

"Hi," I respond robotically. Shaking my head and still holding the door, I ask, "What are you doing here?"

"I was with Ramsey when you called." He shrugs and kicks one of his feet against the door frame. "Came to see if you wanted to get out of the dorms, go for a walk or something."

My spine snaps straight, and I take a step away from him. "I don't need your pity."

He sighs, meeting my eyes again. The grey color looks shiny, almost silver as he speaks. "I also wanted to apologize for what happened at the gym last week. What I said was cruel and I didn't mean it."

I bite my lip, leaning into the door a bit. "Thank you for the apology."

He jerks his chin toward the elevator. "It's nice out tonight. Probably going to be one of the last nicer nights before winter." I hesitate, remembering Bentley warning me to stay away from Harley. "It'd be more fun than sitting on your own in there."

I bite my lip, glancing at the couch. "Fine, let me grab my coat." He nods and waits in the hallway while I slip on my shoes and grab my jean jacket. Locking the door with the key Bentley lent, I walk over to where Harley waits, holding the elevator door. We ride down in silence, his eyes flicking over to mine a couple of times, but we both look away quickly.

When we get out to Ring Road, I point in the opposite direction than the last time we jogged this route. He nods and matches my stride. The other direction leads toward the academic buildings but walking this way will take us through the length of woods that separates the buildings from the athletic fields. With the stars above us and no breeze, it feels nice being out here on a walk. I look over at

Harley who studies our surroundings, and a thought hits me.

My spirits fall. "Ramsey sent you."

Harley's head turns toward me, and he laughs. "No. I was supposed to go with him and a couple girls he met to the show tonight, but I told him there was an emergency at the gym."

I quirk a brow. "What kind of emergency could there be at the gym?" I ask mockingly.

He shrugs, smiling slightly. "I don't know. I'll just tell him someone pulled the fire alarm or something."

We walk a bit more in silence. A few people pass us, but once we pass the last parking lot and enter the part of the road that goes through the woods, it suddenly feels like Harley and I are the only ones around.

"Why would you give up a date to take a walk with me?"

His eyes meet mine again, that wariness back. "I heard your voice on the phone with Ramsey. You were trying to hide how upset you are. I just made up the excuse and drove over here without thinking too much about it."

My heart leaps into my throat.

"What's wrong, Mira?"

I look away from him and at the path we are walking. "What makes you think something is wrong?"

"Mira, come on. I've heard you try to cover up when something's upsetting you a thousand times. I know your voice." I see him side-eye me in my periphery. "I know *you*. What's bothering you?"

I sigh. "It's nothing, Harley. You don't have to look out for me for Ramsey."

Harley reaches out and gently pulls me to a stop, sparks flying under the warmth of his hand on my arm. He holds my gaze as I look up at him. "I was never looking out for you just because of Ramsey, Meerkat. I never actually saw you as my little sister."

My breath hitches in my throat.

"Just his," he adds, letting go of my arm, but not stepping away.

"I don't have any friends," I confess.

Harley's brow furrows. "You have Autumn and Marshall." His jaw clenches a little around Bentley's last name. "And that new girl you brought with you guys to the party. Plus, I saw you with Gwen and her sister there too."

A thrill goes through me at the idea that he watched me at the party. "Aria is Autumn's roommate, and they hit it off so she kind of comes with Autumn by extension now. Gwen is my RA, not exactly a friend. Layla was nice, but I only met her that one time." I look down at my shoes. "It's my freshman year of college and I'm only three weeks in and already on my own watching crappy TV on a Friday night. I always pictured having a whole new group of friends in college and going out to parties or doing girly sleepover hangouts in my dorm with my roommate." I toe my left shoe with my right. "I love Bentley and Autumn and I'm so glad they found people and are having great new experiences, but it feels like I'm missing the boat or something."

Harley's finger curls under my chin and lifts my head, so our eyes meet. "You're always too hard on yourself, Mira. Stop putting so much pressure on everything to turn out exactly how you planned in that head of yours. Things take time." He smiles and everything around him seems to blur out of focus. "You also have Ramsey and the guys whenever you need someone to hang out with." He smirks.

I mock gasp. "The almighty Emerald Grove Ravens would take time out of their busy and important lives to hang out with *me*?" My tone drips with sarcasm and I hope the words disguise the tremble his touch creates.

Harley drops his hand and rolls his eyes.

I smile and wave my hand. "Well, the Ravens minus you."

Harley's eyes cloud over, and his forehead wrinkles. "Why minus me?"

I falter. "Sorry, I'm just used to thinking that in my head. Ever since my fifteenth, it's always been the Ravens, minus you, coming to help me with stuff."

Harley bristles and stares out at the woods around us.

The break in eye contact makes me suddenly feel cold and I flounder. "It's fine! I mean I get why you weren't around after...well what happened, and—

"I'll be around now," he says, gaze back on me and intense.

My brow furrows this time, remembering his words from yesterday. "It's okay, Harley. You don't have to feel some sort of obligation to me because of Ramsey or my parents or anything."

"You still don't get it." Harley runs a hand through his hair.

I squint. "Get what?"

His hand suddenly grips my face, pulling me toward him to seal my lips against his. Shock freezes me in place, and something explodes in the back of my brain as Harley lightly kisses me. I kiss him back, eyes falling closed, and Harley's arm wraps around my waist, dragging me forward and crushing me against his chest. The force of it ramps everything up, my hands fisting his shirt as he works my mouth open, his tongue finding mine. His hand at my waist slides down to squeeze my ass and he bites my bottom lip, making me shudder. He steals my harsh breaths while I slide my hands up into his hair, gripping the strands and tugging. It spurs him to slide the hand on my cheek into my hair and tilt my head further so his tongue can slide deeper into my mouth. I sigh against his lips when his other hand inches up and under my shirt, fingers brushing against the skin of my lower back and causing tingles to spread over my spine.

My overwhelmed senses only feel, taste, *smell* him.

Harley.

A moan rips from my throat as the hand in my hair pulls lightly on the fistful of strands.

Once again, the noise seems to break the spell and he rips his face a few inches away from mine, though he doesn't untangle us any further. I pant, matching his deep gulps of air. His eyes roam my face while I stare at his mouth, imagining his tongue delving other places. Every muscle below my waist clenches at the thought, and I meet his eyes. Heat pools in my jeans and my knees shake a bit.

"Why did you stop?"

He gives me an incredulous look, untangling the hand in my hair, but leaving the one that grips my waist beneath my shirt. "How many times do I have to remind you that you're my best friend's little sister? I'm not supposed to want to kiss you. I'm supposed to—"

I pull a hand out of his hair and clamp it over his mouth. "If you try to say you see me as a sister right now, I will punch you in the nose."

Mirth sparks his eyes, and he shakes his head out from under my hand. "I wasn't going to say that." He pauses a beat before continuing. "But you *are* Ramsey's little sister. As much as I want you…I can't lose him." His hand drops from my waist, and he starts to step back.

13

I grab Harley's wrist in both hands, stopping him. My heart hammers in my chest, pulse racing at the words *I want you.*

"It's okay. I would never jeopardize your friendship with Ramsey." I step closer to him. "But Ramsey's not here. And what he doesn't know, won't hurt him."

Harley looks conflicted, eyes jumping from my lips to my eyes to my hands holding him in place.

"Come on, Harley." I pull him back into the trees and away from the road. Blood pounds in my ears and I brace myself for another rejection as I lay out my last attempt. Harley's eyes stay on mine as he lets me pull him. "Trying to stay away from each other hasn't exactly worked." Once the road is no longer visible, I drop his hand and step into him, reaching up on my tippy toes when his hands land on my hips. "Maybe giving in will get this out of our systems?"

His gaze flicks between my eyes and I hold my breath, waiting for him to make the next move.

"Fuck it," he murmurs, and my stomach somersaults.

Harley backs me up further, pinning me to a tree with

his lower half and pressing his hard on into my stomach. I moan in his ear, and his hand flies back to my hair, pulling my head back just far enough to press his lips to mine, before falling back down to squeeze my hips. I kiss him back, hands gripping his waist as my tongue seeks his out. My nerves fly in every direction, the pendulum swinging too fast for me to keep up with as I lose myself in Harley.

His hands wander up from my hips, both under my shirt, skirting across my stomach to the edge of my bra. He wastes no time passing that barrier and cupping my chest in his massive hands. I throw my hand back as his thumbs find my hard nipples and circle them over the thin cotton. He nips and sucks at my throat as he pinches and squeezes my breasts, making my abs contract harshly and breathing turn erratic. I feel his lips smile against the crook of my neck before he releases one hand and places his finger over the button of my jeans. He pauses, waiting for my head to dip down and our eyes to meet. I nod and he dives forward, kissing me again as he pops my jeans open with one hand. Wasting no time dragging my zipper down, his hand flies into my soaked underwear, index finger gliding across my skin to separate me.

I gasp and Harley's forehead falls against mine.

"Fuck, Mira. You're soaked," he whispers. His finger leisurely circles my clit, making my knees buckle, and I wrap my arms around his neck, closing my eyes as he watches my face up close. His other hand comes back down from my chest and wraps around my waist again to help hold me up.

As his finger leaves my clit, he leans forward and nips my bottom lip again, forcing my eyes to fly open so that I stare into his and he suddenly thrusts one thick finger into me, finding no resistance. Pride covers his face at the gasp I release, and he pulls out only to insert two fingers this time, stretching me a bit. He starts moving in earnest, his thumb pressing and circling my clit as he pumps his fingers in and out of me. The sound is obscene, and my hips chase his hand, toes the only thing touching the ground. My stomach tightens and I clench around him as I start to build. He holds my eyes, as I bite my lip to try to stop the whiny noises escaping the back of my throat.

His lips brush the shell of my ear just as he crooks his fingers inside me, making me buck. I jump when his thumb presses into my clit and rubs side to side, as he whispers, "Come for me, Meerkat."

I lean forward and bite his shoulder to muffle the scream I release as I detonate and soak his hand.

He holds onto me as his fingers continues to lazily pump in and out and I shudder and spasm against him, riding the high that envelops my entire body. My blood sings and my lungs seem to drag in helium as I float on the high of the orgasm.

When I finally stop moving, I release my jaw from his shoulder and lean my head back against the tree, staring up at the stars as my vision swims in and out of focus for a moment. Harley pulls his hand out of my jeans, bringing his fingers up to his mouth. He sticks his index and middle fingers in, sucking me off him, as he holds my gaze, eyes molten and burning through me. A smirk lifts one side of his mouth as he releases his fingers and groans, removing his arm from around my waist. I stare at him, still panting, as he re-zips my jeans and fastens the button. My shirt rode up and got stuck against the inside of my jacket so that half my bra and stomach are on display. Harley grabs the edge of the material and brings it back down, before righting my jacket on my shoulders. With his hands gripping the lapels, he leans forward and gives me a simple sweet kiss before leaning back and smiling.

I return the smile drunkenly, searching his eyes for any hint of regret. They stay clear and steady, still burning with the fire I saw as he watched me come undone. His mouth hangs open slightly, and I like the idea of my taste lingering on his tongue tonight. My stomach clenches.

"My turn," I whisper, and he tilts his head. I reach out and cup the outline of his dick through his jeans, rubbing against him.

He groans and closes his eyes, forehead tipping toward mine. The small move makes me grin as power surges through my veins.

"You don't have to, Mir. I'm fine leaving things here."

I squeeze him and my stomach swoops when another noise of pleasure slips through his lips. I lean forward and whisper, "I'm not," before pecking him swiftly and falling to my knees. The ground is soft beneath me, and I take a moment to be thankful it hasn't rained recently. As it was, I'm probably getting dirt on my jeans, but it'll be easier to wipe off than wet stains when we walk back to West Tower.

Focusing back on the task at hand, I pop the button on his jeans, and slide the zipper down slowly, pressing it in a little so it slides along his cock. His fists flex on either side of me, and I glance up to find his eyes screwed shut.

"Eyes on me, Harley."

His liquid grey gaze meets mine, jaw set.

I smile wolfishly before tugging his jeans and boxers down, just enough for him to spring free. His cock juts out, bobbing a bit before I reach out and squeeze, sliding my fist over his length.

He hisses and I glance up, making sure his eyes still watch me. Leaning forward and holding his gaze, I lick the underside of his head, bringing the tip of my tongue up and over his slit, catching the bead of precum already leaking out. His taste spreads over my tongue and I hum, lips vibrating against his skin. He shudders and I break our eye contact, wrapping my lips around him and slowly sliding down to encase his dick. My eyes shutter closed as the weight of him settles in my mouth and a thrill running up my spine.

I'm about to make Harley Sanders come undone.

I start moving, sucking and savoring while I take more of him in with each pass. I get a rush each time his tip hits the back of my throat. It makes his hips stutter as he holds himself back from thrusting further so with my free hand, I grab one of his and place it on the side of my head. He grips my hair, just holding on, not moving me. His other hand comes to the same spot on the other side of my head, and I release the one I guided, starting to move my mouth faster over his dick. His breathing comes in shakily and the sound of him losing control causes the already soaked state in my underwear to worsen.

With both hands in my hair, he massages my scalp every time he tightens and loosens his grip. I pull back entirely, tilting my head up so that his tip touches my chin. He stares down at me, teeth on display as he grits them.

"I want you to come down my throat," I say, and his eyes shutter closed. His dick twitches against me and I internally crow.

When his eyes open again, his pupils are blown so wide, the grey around the edges looks miniscule.

I kiss his tip. "You're in control. Fuck my throat." His hands falter on either side of my head, so I add, "I trust you."

The words seem to work as I put my lips back around his

cock and he uses his hands to angle my face where he wants. He thrusts forward with his hips, finding a fast rhythm that has him moaning above me. I hold on to his wrists loosely, letting him take the reins and moaning when he thrusts completely in, choking me for a moment as I breathe through my nose. My hips grind against the seam of my jeans when my throat stretches around him, and I close my eyes at the sensation.

He holds himself still before pulling out slowly and then thrusting forward again. I shudder as he picks up speed, pulling my hair a bit and losing all rhythm. Opening my eyes, I look up and release one of his wrists, placing my palm underneath his sac and massaging. He pulls back and groans while his dick jerks in my mouth and salty cum shoots across the back of my tongue. I swallow and suck lightly as he stills, panting my name above me.

Once his hands release my head, I pull my mouth off, wiping my lips and licking some errant cum from my fingertips.

Harley stares down at me, eyes half open and blazing, hands against the tree now, seeming to hold himself up. I shimmy his boxers and jeans back up, tucking his deflating cock in before zipping and buttoning them up. Standing, I end up with his hands on either side of my head and smirk at his foggy, reverent stare. He leans forward and kisses me, slipping his tongue past my lips. We both moan as we taste each other mix, but Harley pulls back first.

"That was not your first time doing that," he muses, hand coming up to cradle the nape of my neck.

I shrug, still smirking. "I've never really dated anyone, but I had a couple friends with benefits."

A shadow seems to fall over Harley's face as his thumb strokes my jaw. "Marshall?" His voice rasps as he asks.

A sharp laugh comes out. "No, never. We tried dating once, but we're really just better as friends."

Harley hums, lips pulling into a lazy smile. "Who then?"

"You want the list?"

Harley scowls and drops his hands, looking around at the trees.

I laugh. "It's not even a handful."

"I don't care how many," he says, looking back at me. "I just want names."

"So what? You can go after them?" I laugh, but it pulls up short when his expression doesn't change.

He shrugs. "Smith has people that would help me."

"Seriously? You are not hunting down every guy who ever touched me."

Harley shrugs and takes a step back. "I'll get the names out of you."

I push my back off the tree, standing up fully. "I don't see how."

His hand shoots out and drags the back of my head forward, so our lips meet once again. The kiss makes me dizzy and ends with him sucking my lip into his mouth and nibbling on it a bit. I whimper and he releases me, smirking. "I don't think it'll be too hard."

He takes my hand, leading me back toward the road as I mutter, "It better be hard," under my breath.

We emerge from the woods, probably looking very obvious, though no one is this far out on campus tonight to see. Harley keeps my hand in his as we continue our walk around Ring Road. The feeling this time is a lot lighter, both of us glancing at the other a few times and holding stares before someone smiles and we continue forward.

I knock into his shoulder a few minutes later, keeping

our hands interlocked between us. "If it makes you feel better, you were my first kiss."

Harley stops, pulling me to a halt next to him. "*That* was your first kiss?"

"Besides elementary school pecks, yeah, that was it on the patio at my party." I shrug, still blissed out from our activities in the woods.

He stares at me before his voice comes out quietly. "I fucked up your first kiss?"

I study his face before shrugging. "You've more than made up for it by now." His eyes roam my face before he nods, and we continue walking.

After a few minutes, I speak up again. "I meant what I said."

He looks over at me quizzically.

"Ramsey doesn't have to know. No one does." I think about Bentley's multiple warnings against being near Harley. "This is just a friends with benefits thing, right? Just scratching the itch so that we don't explode around each other."

He faces forward, considering my words. My heart skipped as I said them, but I know nothing serious can ever happen with us. Not without affecting his relationship with my brother, my parents. I'll take anything I can get right now. I'll deal with the aftermath when it comes.

"Friends with benefits," Harley muses. "Alright, under one condition." I wait. "We resume the training to make sure you can defend yourself if you're ever followed home again."

I breathe a sigh of relief. "Deal," I say.

"Great. I'll pick you up tomorrow morning then." Harley stops and I realize we are back in front of West Tower. No one is around, probably either tucked away inside or still out since the night is young. I don't see Bentley's car in the usual spot he parks it in, though a wine colored Toyota is occupying it, so he could just be parked somewhere else in the lot.

I push Harley's shoulder lightly. "You're not leaving me on the ground this time. See, already an improvement." I chuckle and he looks down at me, unimpressed.

He leans forward, hand at the back of my head again. "I'm sorry about that, by the way. I shouldn't have dropped you, let alone left you there that night."

I smile, leaning up on my tippy toes to whisper. "It's okay, you'll just have to make it up to me tomorrow."

Harley groans, eyes closing before he drags me forward and kisses me chastely. "Go inside, Mira," he says against my mouth before releasing me and stepping back.

I smirk before turning on my heel and heading for the doors. Once past them, I turn around to see Harley standing exactly where I left him, watching me. My smile widens and he shakes his head before nodding his chin at me. I roll my eyes and head to the elevator to return to Bentley's suite.

14

Harley drums his fingers against the steering wheel as I walk out to the truck. Bentley commented on me being in a good mood when he got back from his date, but I woke up with moths in my gut.

What if Harley already regrets everything?

The thought kept bouncing around in my head as I got ready. When Harley texted saying he was downstairs, my pulse raced as the moths took flight, and all tried to escape my throat at the same time.

Getting into the truck, Harley smiles at me before heading to the gym. His music is turned up and he hums along as he drives. I glance over at him a few times, playing with the comfort scrunchie on my wrist, but my mind draws a blank on what to say right now. He seems in a good mood, but he hasn't said anything, didn't touch me when I got in the truck.

He parks in front of the gym and turns off the engine, grabbing his bag from the back and getting out without a word or glance toward me. The moths start to eat me from the inside out as I grab my bag off the floor and put my hand out to open the door. My hand falls through empty air though, my body following after it as I pitch to the side. I meant to shoulder the door open, but the door seems to no longer be there. As I flail to try to right myself, Harley's hand on my shoulder stops my fall and I look into his eyes as he tries to hold in a laugh.

"You always throw yourself out of the car when someone opens the door for you?"

I sit up and get out, feet first this time and stand before him. "Considering the last time I was in your truck, I opened my own doors, I wasn't really expecting it."

Harley chuckles and backs up so I can walk around him. He closes the door and leads the way inside, unlocking the gym and going around to turn on the lights. I drop my bag off behind the front desk and follow him to the storage room to move the big rolled up mats we used last time. Harley still seems way more relaxed around me this morning but says nothing more and when he bumps into me to get to the other side of the mats, I seem to be the only one who needs a second to clear my head.

I don't know what I expected. Something different. But once we move the mats into the training room, Harley goes right back to how we were before yesterday. We break down one of the defense moves, and he has me repeat the steps in slow motion over and over again. Every time he reaches out and corrects my stance or shows me how to get more power, I hold my breath until his fingers leave my skin, memories of last night filtering through my head.

He seems unaffected, moving back each time and saying, "Again."

At some point, I lose myself in the training, my brain

turning off and just following his instructions as we run through another move for twenty minutes.

"Enough," Harley calls, glancing at the clock on the wall. "Take a break." He puts a water in my hand and then walks over to his bag, rummaging around for something. I sip the water, pacing a little bit to calm myself down. If this new deal between Harley and me makes me this restless all the time, I'm going to need to figure out some new parameters for seeing him. I feel jumpy and just want to ask him what is going on with us but don't want to come off whiny.

I take a deep breath. Friends with benefits. This is just the friends part. It will take some getting used to.

"You're improving," Harley calls and I turn to find him only a foot behind me. "Did you keep up practicing over the week?"

I shake my head. "Not really. I've been walking more than I did at home, having to get to classes and West Tower and such, but otherwise nothing new." I shrug.

He nods. "We'll start running again and you'll notice more of a difference in a few weeks." He stares at me for a minute, the look in his eyes changing. "Help me put away the mats?"

Heat rises in my cheeks at his look, and I simply nod before swallowing. We roll up the two mats quickly before lifting them and carrying them out to the storage room. Harley opens the door for me, holding the mat over his shoulder with one hand.

I walk in, carrying my mat in front of me with both arms wrapped around it and throw it down on the pile in the back of the room. Turning around, I find Harley right there, his mat thrown to the side. His arms loop around my waist and he pulls me against his chest. The door closes behind him and for a moment we are in complete darkness before he flicks a switch on the nearest wall and then reaches down to lock the door.

I grin up at him as he stares down at me with a sly look. "I think I remember you saying something about making things up to you yesterday?"

"Do we have time?" I ask, staring at his lips. My voice sounds breathy, and I clear my throat.

His grin widens. "Why do you think I stopped us thirty minutes early? We have about that much time until my employees start showing up."

I return his grin before craning up to kiss him.

His mouth descends onto mine and he backs me up until my ass hits a wall. The kiss makes me lightheaded and an ache lower in my stomach replaces the jittery feeling from earlier. I kiss him back, lips moving fervently with his, as my hands slide into his hair once more. The strands are soft and easily tangle around my fingers as I grip onto him. His hands find their way underneath my shirt and start skimming across my skin, lifting the material with them. We part to breathe and so he can rip the tee shirt the rest of the way off, leaving me in my bright red sports bra. He pauses, taking me in, eyes seeming to try to light me on fire and coming a hairsbreadth away from succeeding.

"Always fucking red," he murmurs, before pouncing on me again, this time avoiding my mouth and running his teeth along my jaw. I tip my head back to grant him better access and gasp when his fingers start pulling down the bra's zipper at the center of my chest. His mouth moves down my throat, tongue leaving a wet trail that makes me shiver as the open air hits it. When the zipper ends its descent, my boobs spill from the bra unsupported. Harley's waiting hands envelop them, the feeling of his skin on mine making me keen, hands weakly clawing at the shirt covering his chest.

His thumbs immediately start playing with my nipples as he squeezes my chest and his mouth moves further south, trailing nips and kisses across the swell of my chest. I lean heavily into the wall, letting it support me as his mouth encloses around my right nipple and he sucks harshly before biting down. I cry out, drenching my leggings. I forwent underwear this morning in the hopes of things ending up somewhat like this.

His eyes watch my face as he releases my right nipple and blows on it, making me squirm at the icy sensation. At some point, I fisted my hand in his hair and now I pull, trying to move his mouth to the other side.

He chuckles, and whispers, "Patience," against my skin.

I pull his hair more forcefully and huff, earning a squeeze at my waist.

"I dreamt all night about tasting you again. I'm taking my time today, Mira." His mouth bites and sucks across the valley of my chest before he reaches my left nipple, rolling the tip of his tongue around it slowly. I drop my head back against the wall, breath sharp. He chuckles again, before taking my nipple between his teeth and rolling it while licking harshly.

I gasp, my free hand clawing against the wall behind me as I rub my thighs together. The ache between them is becoming unbearable and I need him to do something *soon*.

Harley stands up suddenly, stepping back to pull my bra down my shoulders and tosses it behind him with my shirt. I reach for the hem of his shirt, but he catches my wrist and places it back against the wall beside me.

"No fair," I hiss, and one side of his mouth raises.

"Patience," he repeats. I stomp my foot, and he raises an eyebrow. His hands hook into my leggings on either side of my hips, and he forces them down to my knees in one rough tug. Working them the rest of the way off, I end up bare before him. He studies me for a moment before shaking his head and putting his hands back on my hips. He maneuvers me off the wall, pushing me down onto a mat already unrolled and laid out.

I raise an eyebrow once I am lying down, Harley hovering over me. "Did you set this up beforehand?"

Harley shrugs with a sheepish grin. "I might have hoped we would get time for something like this." He leans down and kisses me deeply, before pulling back and searching my eyes. "I've always wanted to fuck at the gym." I stare back at him, unsure how to respond, when he adds, "Last time we trained, I couldn't stop thinking about dragging you in here."

My heart stutters at the confession while Harley's head dips and he kisses down my neck. I writhe underneath him when he nips the swell of my breast, and my breathing shallows when his hands part my legs before coming up to part my lower lips.

He kisses his way down my stomach after sucking and licking the skin on my chest. My nipples ache to be touched, but he leaves them alone, probably leaving hickeys around them with how brutal his mouth feels. I can't help squirming. By comparison, his mouth turns gentle as he pecks and licks a path down my torso to my core. His fingers lazily circle my clit, eliciting sparks of pleasure at random intervals when he presses down. At my hips, he stops to lightly bite the squishy flesh over my right hip bone. My back arches off the mat and I cry out at the sensation, one of his fingers entering me at the same time. I feel him smile against my hip and then his mouth and fingers disappear. I look down just as his hands push my thighs further apart. He stares down, pupils blown wide and eyes blazing as he lays himself down, aligning his face with my center.

"You still trust me?" he asks.

I inhale sharply at the feel of his breath across my dampened skin. Unable to speak, I nod emphatically.

In an instant, his mouth is on me, tongue laving against me. He takes his time exploring as I writhe beneath him, eyes closed and panting. He avoids my clit and circles my entrance with the stiff tip of his tongue. I shudder and one of his hands slides up to the center of my torso, palm flat and pressing down, while his other arm bands over my hips to stop me from bucking up against his face. My hands move back to his hair.

Harley sucks my clit into his mouth and nibbles, making me drench his chin. I clench around nothing, trying to maneuver his tongue to my entrance. His teeth graze my clit one more time before he releases it and my hips, two of his fingers slowly entering me. I clench around them once they are fully embedded, trying to pull them deeper inside. He laughs against my skin and the feeling has me arching against the hand still holding me against the mat. He devours my clit as he starts slowly pumping his fingers in and out. My hips stutter to the rhythm, grinding down on his hand and face as I cry out. He alternates between mouthing my clit and drinking up the juices flowing out of me and down his wrist.

After a few more strokes of his tongue, my orgasm hits, my vision going white as heat and bliss fly through me at competing speeds. My mouth opens in a silent cry and my ears start to ring as everything becomes focused around him diving further in between my thighs to catch everything spilling forth. His fingers disappear as his tongue dives inside, prolonging everything.

I fall back against the mat a minute later, attempting to catch my breath as he leans up, eyes shining along with his lips. My head lolls to see him and once he holds my gaze, his tongue comes out and cleans the excess off around his mouth. His lips pull up in a smug smile once he's done.

"How was that?" he asks and creeps back up my body, placing his hands on either side of my head to hold himself up. I can feel him hard against my hip. "Make up for some things?"

I throw my arms weakly around his neck. "You can drop me anytime if that is part of the apology." He laughs, one hand sliding up and down my side as I shudder a bit from aftershocks.

He leans forward and kisses me, tongue delving into my mouth. I taste myself, eagerly pulling him closer for more.

"You taste divine," he whispers when we pull away, my breathing still irregular.

My hands slip from his neck, sliding down over his chest to stop at the hem of his shirt again. I tug a bit, hinting at what I want, and he reaches back behind his neck to rid his body of the shirt. Tossing it behind him, I explore the newly exposed planes of his body, fingers gliding across his skin and pressing in between the outlines of muscle. When I skim his abs, he inhales sharply, everything contracting beneath my fingertips. I smile, fingers falling to the waistband of his shorts. His dick presses into me against the front of the grey nylon material. I pull the waistband back from his skin, my hand sliding into his shorts. Finding him bare beneath them, I grin as I grip him and move my hand along his length. His eyes close above me and I watch his face as I play around with different pressures and speeds. After a minute, he pulls my hand away, pinning it beside my head.

"If you don't stop, I'm going to come." He nips my bottom lip before releasing my hand and reaching into the pocket of his shorts. He pulls out a condom and holds it up before me. I stare at it for a second before my eyes flick over to his. "Only if you want to," he whispers.

I wrap a leg around his waist and breathe my reply. "Yes."

He smirks before leaning down to kiss me, tongue immediately invading my mouth. One of his hands tangles in my hair while the other one reaches down to tear his shorts off. I help push them down with my feet and we continue kissing as he opens and rolls the condom on. We don't break the kiss until I feel the dull head of his cock at my entrance. He pulls back to stare at me, watching my face as he slowly pushes into me. Something inside my chest swells and my inner walls clench making him groan and continue. I feel a slight stretch once he's fully inside, but the feeling subsides while he holds himself there, waiting for me to adjust. I nod after a moment, and he pulls out only slightly before thrusting back in hard. I gasp, eyes falling closed, and he repeats the action, lips back on mine while his tongue mimics the thrust of his hips in my mouth. I claw at his back, and he starts to pick up speed, pulling out almost entirely before snapping back into me. My stomach starts to contract, another climax building and my legs stiffen, thighs gripping into his hips.

He pulls out entirely and my eyes fly open, about to protest, but Harley flips me over too quickly to say anything. My chest winds up flat against the mat, while he angles my hips before plunging back in from behind. The angle feels deeper, and I cry out, the sound trailing off into a moan as he picks up his rhythm from before. He threads his fingers through mine, chest pressed to my back, harsh breathing in my ear. My hips follow his tempo, crashing against him in synchronicity. We chase our peaks together, mine hitting a few thrusts later as his cock pounds against the spot inside me that makes me see stars.

"Fuck, Mira," he utters before groaning as he comes while I clench around him. He stills, leaning his full weight into me for a few moments as we come down. His breath fans against the back of my neck, sending chills down my spine as I shake a bit underneath him.

He wraps an arm around my middle, falling to the side so I am spooned against him, still inside me. He starts to go soft, the sensation weird in my over-sensitized vagina, but not unpleasant. His face burrows into the crook of my neck, and I close my eyes, feeling spent from the combined workout and sex.

I laugh a moment later and his head pops up. "Something funny?" he asks.

I nod, turning so I lay on my back. He slips out of me as I do and reaches down to remove the condom and tie it off before looking back at me expectantly.

"I was disappointed when you didn't touch me in the car this morning. I thought you might have gone home and reconsidered everything." I smirk. "Clearly not."

He rolls his eyes, laying his head back down so he holds me from the side, tucking his face into the crook of my neck. "I just want you for your body," he murmurs, but the words bounce around inside my head.

I know this isn't just physical for me, but is it for him? He's more caring toward me outside of sex than any of the previous guys I slept with, but maybe that's just because he's Ramsey's best friend? The lines feel muddy, and I can't tell anymore if it's me making them unclear or him.

His head whips up suddenly and he glances at his wrist.

"We should get dressed. Grace will probably be here in a few minutes."

I start to sit up and we detangle ourselves, handing each other our clothes as we collect and find them. I run my fingers through my hair once I am dressed and his hands push mine out of the way from behind, running through my hair to work out some of the tangles and smooth the back. I take off my scarlet scrunchie and hand it to him, letting him gather and contain my tresses in a messy ponytail. I turn around and do the same to him, a smile on my face.

He kisses me once we are done and then takes my hand and pulls me from the storage room. We break off, him heading back to the training room to get his bag, while I walk over to the front desk and collect mine.

Harley is already back at my side as I place it on my shoulder. "I'm driving you home from now on, so tell Marshall to head back if he's here."

I smile. "He's not. I figured you would offer if we didn't get into another fight."

Harley's eyes narrow, opening his mouth to say something, but the front door opens. Derek walks in.

"Hey boss, what are you doing here? Isn't today your day off?" He glances over at me, his face transforming from shock to confusion.

Harley nods. "I'm giving Mira some personal training time before the gym opens. Works better for each of our schedules."

I cough to cover the laugh that bubbles up. Getting up this early was not what I would have chosen if I was actually one of his clients.

Harley places his hand on my back and pinches me, forcing me to cover my reaction with a wide smile. "Thought Grace was opening today?"

Derek glances between us, before his eyes land back on Harley. "She was, but she needed to switch to later for some reason. I didn't ask too many questions since the earlier shift works better for me today too." He looks over at me and winks. "Frees up my evening."

Harley's hand creeps up until his arm rests over my shoulders and I can feel him tense beside me. "That's fine, just let me know next time if you're trading shifts." I assume he was trying for causal, but the words came out through clenched teeth, so I place my hand on the small of his back, rubbing circles into it. He relaxes a fraction and unclenches his jaw before speaking again. "We were just heading out, so I'll see you tomorrow."

Derek nods, heading off to start opening the gym, but not before glancing back at us as Harley ushers me out the door.

"What was that about?" I say as I close the door to his truck. Harley kept his arm around me the whole walk over and then abruptly dropped it to go over to his side.

"I didn't like him leering at you." Harley throws the truck into reverse and backs up, tension still rolling off him.

I pull my seat belt on, looking down. "He was just flirting. What's it matter if we're just sleeping together?" I turn back to watch his reaction.

Harley's eyes flash to mine, darting over my face, before he turns back to the road and turns out of the parking lot. "It doesn't. Just habit from Ramsey wanting to protect you."

Hiding behind my brother again. I sigh, sinking back into the truck's seat. Harley stays silent the whole drive back to campus, not looking over at me once.

When he idles on West Tower's curb, I grab my bag and start to open the door, but Harley's hand lands on my arm, stopping me. I turn back to him, but he freezes, just staring at me. I can see him trying to figure out what he wants to say, and I know whatever it is, it won't be something I want to hear.

"See you tomorrow morning for a run?" I offer.

The wrinkles in his forehead clear, and he releases my arm. "Sounds good. I know you have eight a.m.'s, so we can skip Monday and do more training Tuesday after your ten."

I startle. "How do you know my class schedule?"

Harley's face heats and he looks away, putting his hands on the steering wheel. "Asked Ramsey for it so I could figure out how to fit training in around your classes." My eyes widen as he continues, "Told him I wanted to know it in case you had an emergency, and he was in class."

I smile and roll my eyes. "How thoughtful."

He smirks, looking back over at me. "I'll see you tomorrow, Meerkat."

I open the door and hop out, leaning back in to say, "I'll be sure not to wear underwear again." His eyes widen and I shut the door, walking inside without looking back.

Harley

Ramsey yells at me to move and shakes me from my distracted thoughts. I quickly maneuver my character out of the way with the controller in my hand. Royal weaves back and forth on the couch next to me, mimicking his character's movements as his tongue pokes out the side of his mouth. Ramsey sits on the chair to my left, mashing buttons while he yells at the TV. Tanner lays out on the carpet in front of the entertainment center, a book held over his face.

My character dies on the screen, and I huff when Ramsey yells, "Come on, man!"

I thought starting my little arrangement with Mira would lower the amount of time I spend thinking about her, slaking the lust that built up. But this is the third time today I've been distracted remembering taking her against my desk at the gym a few days ago. We've been fucking for weeks now, and I can't seem to *stop* thinking about her at this point. I've changed my work schedule, so I'll be available more when she isn't in class. It resulted in us having sex all over campus and all over my gym whenever we're together.

I set my controller down, sighing and running a hand through my hair.

"Something distracting you, Har?" Tanner calls from the floor.

"Probably thinking about Cheryl's tits," Ramsey says, still manically concentrating on the game. "She basically slapped him in the face with them today when he was adjusting one of the treadmill belts."

I cringe, remembering the incident. I knelt over a machine and Cheryl called my name, making me look up right at her pushed out chest. I thought Mira was going to murder the girl from the next treadmill over. I convinced her to get a membership at the gym and start running there on days our schedules didn't line up. She begrudgingly agreed when I argued that it would help explain why she was at the gym if Ramsey ever caught her there in the morning. He was there this morning, saying hi to Mira before going over to the free weights to do his usual routine.

I had to reprimand Cheryl in front of everyone, mostly to stop Mira from making any move, but also because she's started to get a little too bold with her advances. The next incident would be a written warning and anything after that would definitely mean termination. I rub my temples, hoping the verbal warning is enough to stop things so I don't have to lose another semi-decent employee.

Royal gets killed and Ramsey follows quickly afterward. "Fuck," Royal hisses, sagging into the couch. "You've been shit tonight," he says, pointing at me. "What's got you distracted?"

"Fuck off," I grumble.

"Definitely a chick," Ramsey leans forward and snags

the beer he abandoned on the coffee table. "Only thing that gets him this riled."

I glance away, thinking of Mira and feeling guilt gnaw my organs. Ramsey might be laughing and joking around but if he knew I was sitting here, picturing Mira on her knees, he'd turn murderous.

Royal shakes his head. "Well get your shit together. I want to win one of these." He grabs his controller, loading up another game. I sigh, picking up my own controller and selecting the same character I always play as. Tanner flips a page as the game starts.

I try to stay focused, try to follow the random commands Ramsey screams out between expletives, but my mind randomly flips to Mira whispering *more* roughly in my ear as I fucked her against the tree we first hooked up against. She dragged me into the woods on a morning run and walked over to the tree asking if I knew where we were. When I rolled my eyes at her before quickly pinning her against the bark, she'd only taken a second to catch her breath before wolfishly grinning and shoving her hand into my joggers.

I've started bringing two or three condoms every time I know I'll be seeing her. The few times I was without ended in the best blowjobs I've ever received, but I like having the option to bury myself in her whenever possible.

My dick stirs in my sweats at the thought, just as my character's head gets blown off on the screen.

"What the fuck, dude?" Ramsey yells as his and Royal's characters soon follow suit. He throws his controller at me, missing by a mile, before getting up and stalking into the kitchen to get another beer.

Royal shoves my shoulder. "You fucking suck."

I pull my phone out, finding no notifications and opening my messages to see the last thing I sent Mira. It had been a *see you soon* text from a few days ago when I left to pick her up for training. She never responds to those but always stands on the curb outside West Tower when I pull up. A smile ghosts my lips as my fingers hover over my phone screen.

I glance at the clock just visible over the top of Tanner's book. Barely after eight. She should be in her dorm, probably studying or binge watching something in her living room if Janette isn't around.

I haven't seen her dorm yet, but I've wondered several times if it looks similar or completely different to her room back home. April helped decorate it, adding a lot of blues and creams, but I know if Mira had spoken up, red would be the theme.

I stand, grabbing my jean jacket off the back of Ramsey's chair and shrugging it on.

"Where you heading?" Royal asks, looking at me over the back of the couch.

"He's going to go fuck whoever it is messing with his head," Ramsey says, walking back in and flopping down on the chair without looking over at me. Royal shrugs, turning back to the TV as they load up another game without me.

I grab my keys and leave the house, jogging over to my truck and pulling away from the house the moment the engine turns over.

I drive the five minutes down the road to the West Tower lot, dick hardening the whole way. I keep picturing Mira spread out beneath me; hair splayed over her pillow, looking decadent against ruby red sheets. Whenever I'm around Mira, everything seems to drip red.

For all the times we've been together, we have yet to make it to a bed considering our incognito situation. I'm praying her roommate isn't home, but also figure Mira won't really care that much if she sees me show up since they don't really get along. Not like Janette even knows who I am to Mira or Ramsey for that matter.

Slamming into park, I pause, looking up at the building. I start to wonder if this is a good idea, but picturing Mira's smile when she opens the door to find me on the other side has me opening the door and climbing out. I adjust things so that anyone I come across won't immediately figure out how aroused I am and then head inside, following a group through the doors when they swipe their IDs then breaking off toward the elevator.

My vision seems to zone in on the door to Mira's suite and I knock quickly, stepping back and waiting. A few moments of dead air pass, and I glance around before knocking again. No sound comes from the other side, and I rub the back of my neck, not wanting to get caught standing outside Mira's door by Gwen or someone. I pull my phone out.

> What are you up to?

The three gray dots appear almost instantly.

AMIRIA ADAMS

> Did you just send me a "you up" text at 8pm on a Thursday?

I roll my eyes, walking back to the elevator.

> Well I know you're not in your dorm since that's where I am.

The dots appear and disappear. I add another quick text, hoping it will provoke her response.

> You better not be at Marshall's right now.

AMIRIA ADAMS

> Not like I knew you'd be randomly showing up tonight.

I huff out a breath through my nose, entering the elevator.

> Tell me if I need to go up to his room or back down to the parking lot right now.

AMIRIA ADAMS

> I'm out right now Harley.

I sigh and lean back against the wall of the elevator. I punch the ground floor button.

> Out where?

Mira has been hanging out more with Marshall, Autumn, and Aria, even pulling Layla into the group a couple times. I was so proud of her when she told me she joined the art club to get out more and back into drawing regularly. She's settling more into life here and part of me itches to make sure I stay part of it.

AMIRIA ADAMS

> A bar.

I go through the roster of bars downtown that will serve

underage students. There are three popular ones, so I walk over to my truck, coming up with a plan. I smirk, knowing it will piss Mira off. Angry Mira is a toss-up but if she isn't angry enough to send me home after, the end of the night will be fantastic. I send two texts quickly then head downtown.

HARLEY

See you soon.

I stare at the words again, a thrill zinging through my blood. Harley sent it twenty minutes ago and still has not responded to my frantic response.

What are you going to do?

Bentley nudges my shoulder, quirking his eyebrows when I glance over at him. I shake my head, putting my phone down and tuning back in. Layla sits on the barstool next to me, leaning on the high-top we snagged when we saw her and Janette here. Axel tells a story about how he broke his ankle jumping off a roof. Autumn listens intently across from me while Aria looks around, people watching and fidgeting a bit with her fingers. I think she's nervous since this is our first time using the fakes Bentley got us online. We already passed the bouncer at the door though, so I feel comfortable.

My phone pulls my attention down to the tabletop again, flipping it over to see that I still have no new notifications.

Is he coming here?

That makes no sense. He doesn't want anyone to know we're hooking up and just showing up here would raise some questions. Especially with Bentley. Lying to him about hanging out with Harley the last few weeks has been eating me alive. I hate not being able to talk to him about everything I've been thinking and feeling. But the moment I tell him, he's going to be mad that I lied on top of being mad that I'm still around Harley. I feel the need to put my forehead on the table, but tipping anyone off that I am panicking will only make things worse.

Instead, I throw on a smile and laugh with everyone else at the end of Axel's story.

Autumn rolls her eyes as we quiet. "That was completely your own fault."

"No way! It was the squirrel's!" Axel yells. Autumn shakes her head, sipping her drink. "If it hadn't charged me, I wouldn't have fell!"

Janette snorts. "Squirrels don't charge people."

Axel puts his hand on the back of Autumn's chair to lean over her and say something back, but the bell over the bar's door rings and my head swivels. My gut clenches when I see Harley walk in. The brief excitement dies as I register Ramsey, Tanner, and Royal walking in behind him. All of their eyes find me and they head over, Ramsey passing Harley and reaching our table first.

"What are you doing here?" he demands.

Harley comes to stand behind his shoulder while Tanner veers off to the bar. Royal sidles up on the other side of the table. I feel Bentley at my back, ready to step in if needed.

Harley crosses his arms over his chest.

"Hanging out. What the hell are you doing here?" I sit up straighter, swiveling the stool to fully face my brother.

"You're not old enough to hang out in bars, Amiria." My face heats and Ramsey glances around the table. "None of you are, actually."

"Don't chastise them. Like you never drank before twenty-one." I roll my eyes. "You're being hypocritical." My voice rises with indignation, and I feel Bentley's hand land on my shoulder as Ramsey's eyes blaze. Harley leans forward; eyes trained on Bentley's hand. I shrug it off.

"That's different," Ramsey says.

I open my mouth to argue but he cuts me off.

"I didn't have anyone there to stop me from making mistakes. You have me, so you're not going to do the same stupid shit I did."

I inhale indignation, anger swirling in my chest, ready to rush out my mouth.

Autumn cuts me off this time. "Oh please." We turn to her, and she glares at Ramsey. "Because sitting here in a bar having one drink is really going to ruin her life."

Tanner walks up with three beers, giving one to Royal and one to Harley. "Figured Ramsey would be dragging Mini-Adams home," he murmurs to Royal.

"He will not be!" I shout and Ramsey's furious gaze flicks back to me. His fists clench along with his jaw as he takes a step toward me. I hold my ground, but Harley steps around Ramsey and into my line of sight.

"Drink a beer, dude. Cool down, hang out." I lean around Harley's back to see my brother's reaction. He takes a deep breath and grabs the beer from Harley, chugging half. "School's stressing you out too much. You're burning out with all your pre-med classes and TAing."

Autumn jolts in her seat, staring over at Ramsey.

Harley turns so that he can look between Ramsey and me. "I'll take Mira home. The girl I was supposed to meet never showed up anyway. You guys stay and have fun."

Bentley leans forward to argue, but I grab his arm. "Whatever," I say, shaking my head at Bentley and getting off the stool. I grab my purse and start to storm out of the bar. Harley says something to the group before following me out. I look back at the door, finding Bentley staring after us with furrowed brows.

Once on the sidewalk outside, I turn left, heading toward campus. I can feel Harley following. My phone buzzes in my pocket.

BENTLEY

We're getting coffee tomorrow and talking.

I sigh.

Sounds good.

Harley grabs my arm, suddenly steering me to the right and down a side alley. "Truck's this way," he murmurs.

I yank my arm out of his grip and stop, making him turn to face me. I push his chest, moving him all of two inches. "You tattled on me to *Ramsey*?"

"You shouldn't be hanging out at bars, Mira." The words are weak. Harley puts his hands up in a surrendering gesture.

"Do not talk down to me, Harley! I know for a fact you and Ramsey went to bars and partied back in *high school* so don't act like I'm committing some great moral sin." I poke his chest, on my tippy toes as my voice rises.

"Okay, okay." He wraps his arms around my waist, the shadows of the alley shrouding us from passing visibility. "I don't care if you drink or go to bars. I just wanted to see you tonight and thought this was a good idea."

I pull away from him, his arms dropping and hurt flashing in his eyes. "You thought the best way to get me alone with you was to start a fight between me and my brother?"

Harley winces. "When you say it like that, it sounds worse than it did in my head. I figured Ramsey would just send you home." He shrugs and I can see in his face that he wasn't prepared for me to be this angry.

"Ah, yes, because I take orders from Ramsey. Stupid plan, Harley." I turn and walk out of the alley, turning back to the sidewalk that leads back to campus. Wrapping my arms around myself, I combat the cool breeze.

"Mira." His voice pleads me to stop.

I keep walking.

Harley jogs to catch up and stops right in front of me, making me bump into him. His hands shoot out and stop me from falling backward. "I'm sorry. I don't know what I'm doing here."

I murmur, "*clearly,*" under my breath.

Harley ignores it. "I wanted to see you tonight and I couldn't exactly walk in and drag you out."

I pull out of his grip again and throw my hands up. "Did the idea of texting me and asking if I wanted to hang out tonight even cross your mind?" We both glance around, realizing at the same time that I am now yelling in the street.

"Let me drive you home and you can keep yelling at me in the truck, Mir."

I close my eyes, reigning in the white-hot anger that wants to lash out. I feel Harley step closer.

"Please," he whispers. "I really am sorry."

I sigh and open my eyes. "Fine." I turn and walk back down the alley, coming out to the small parking lot in the back. Harley walks over to his truck and opens the passenger door for me. I hop in, slam my seatbelt in place, and fold my arms in the time it takes Harley to round the front and get in. He glances at me as we pull out of the lot, knee bouncing.

We ride in silence from there, my phone buzzing in my pocket a couple minutes later. I fish it out, finding another text from Bentley. I send off a reply to placate him.

Harley side-eyes me as he drives. "That Ramsey?"

"No." I shake my head. "Bentley just wanted to make sure I made it back safe."

Harley stiffens. "What'd you say?"

I put my phone down, turning toward him. "That I was fine, Harley. Why?" I ask, exasperated.

He shrugs, steering with one hand on the wheel, his other elbow on the ledge of the door. He rests his chin on that hand and leans away from me. "Just know you don't want Marshall to know about us, so I was curious what you told him." He stops at a red light and meets my eyes before adding, "You know you're safe with me, right?" I nod. "I wouldn't have let anything happen to you, even if you had been mad enough to walk all the way back."

I look away from him. "I know that, Harley." My heart constricts at his words. He's slowly been saying more things like this the past few weeks, but then my mind replays the words he said that day in the gym.

I only want you for your body.

This is just supposed to be sex, a way to purge the lust

between us, at least for him. I have to keep reminding myself that is still his goal. I can't get my hopes up.

"I think I'm going to tell Bentley about what's going on with us tomorrow."

Harley chews his lip.

"He won't say anything to Ramsey, and I'm tired of hiding it from him. He won't be happy, but it's my life." I sit up straighter, feeling lighter after making the decision. I turn to fully face Harley. "Don't *ever* use Ramsey against me like that again."

Harley slouches, looking sheepish.

"I am actively hiding our situation from him for both of our benefit, and I would never use it or Ramsey against you. Do me the same courtesy."

Harley nods. "I know you wouldn't, Mira. I'm sorry, I shouldn't have done that."

I nod and face forward again. "And stop getting jealous about Bentley. I already told you we're just friends. Nothing's ever going to happen with him."

"Never say never," Harley mutters.

I roll my eyes.

"Friendships make the best foundation for a relationship." He pulls on his bottom lip, eyes strictly facing forward as he drives.

I laugh and he glances over at me. "Not with Bentley. We went on a few dates and even tried to hook up one time. It just isn't there. He's one of the loves of my life, but it's only platonic for us."

Harley nods, turning onto campus. "Why didn't you date anyone in high school?"

I shrug. "It felt weird to try to date someone seriously when I was hung up on you."

Harley sits up, eyebrows furrowing. "Seriously?"

I shrug again, cheeks hot with my admission. "You asked." A moment passes, and I feel the tension in the truck rise.

"You slept with other people though?"

I nod. "You weren't interested and made it pretty obvious. I liked fooling around with some of the guys that hit on me. But anytime I tried to make things more serious, it felt wrong to string them along."

Harley nods, pulling up to West Tower and parking in the lot. He turns toward me once the engine is off. "I didn't stay away because I wasn't interested."

I roll my eyes and smirk. "Yeah, you've made that pretty obvious."

He smiles back, the soft look in his eyes making my chest ache. "Can I come up? I haven't gotten to see your dorm yet."

I bite my lip, glancing at my dorm window. "You sure? What if someone sees you?"

Harley gets out of the truck and comes around to open my door. "Ramsey is at a bar downtown. Everyone else who could catch us is there with him. I want to see your room." He holds his hand out to me. His smile makes my heart twist, but my stomach falls a bit at his words.

I ignore that feeling and take his hand. He pulls me from the truck, and we walk to the elevator. The moment the doors slide closed, my nerves skyrocket. Harley never commented on my room at home, though he'd been there several times when we grew up. I try to remember if the suite is clean, knowing Janette prefers it tidy but worried she suddenly left a bunch of clutter around. I know my desk is messy and a bunch of clothes cover my bed from when I went through my closet trying to decide what to wear tonight.

Harley squeezes my hand, glancing over at me with a grin as the doors open to my floor. He pulls me from the elevator and down the hall. I sigh, dropping his hand and digging around in my bag for my keys.

"I didn't think I'd have company tonight, so it's not exactly tidy," I say, sliding the key into the knob.

"Just open the door, Meerkat."

I push the door open, my breath hitching a bit as he walks past me. Throwing my bag down on the couch, I hang my keys on the hook by the door. Harley stands in the center of the room, glancing around. He wears a small smile as he takes in the little details of the room. The little cactus on the coffee table. The red lunar painting on the wall by the bathroom. The fuzzy blanket slung over the back of a couch.

"Most of it is just the stuff the suite came with, but I added the moon painting." I point it out. Janette was out when I came home with it after getting praised by my professor for the piece. I put it up in the common space on a whim and Janette never said anything. It makes me smile when I'm in the room, having something of mine up in my first home away from my parents' house.

Harley walks up to it, leaning in to study the details.

It's a chunk acrylic paint piece and I spent way too long stressing over each of the craters and shading while staring at my reference picture. My prof gave me simple praise, but it made me beam. It felt like I accomplished something, getting that recognition.

Watching Harley stare at it, I fidget with my wrist scrunchie.

"You painted this?" He glances back at me for a second. I mumble *mmhmm* and he steps away, walking back over to stand in front of me. "You're amazing."

I roll my eyes. "It's a painting of the moon, not the Mona Lisa, Har."

Harley shrugs and cups my face. He gives me a quick kiss before pulling back when I try to deepen it. "That your room?" He points over his shoulder at my door. There is a whiteboard on the door where I doodled some stuff and throw up notes to Janette on the weekends about where I am. I still don't know if she reads them.

I nod and his hand falls away from my face. He winks before walking over to my door and disappearing inside. I close my eyes as my heart rate speeds up. Taking a deep breath, I follow him.

17

Harley

T he room screams Mira and that makes the feeling I sometimes get with her slice through my chest. The deep maroon duvet sits crumpled and bunched at the end of the bed, looking plush and comfy. Her black sheets underneath match the pillowcases. Clothes scatter her bed, some inside out. She squeezes past me, where I stand just inside the threshold and starts tidying, folding some into a dresser and hanging others up in the closet.

Her desk hosts textbooks and papers intermingled with paints and brushes. A little tabletop easel sits in one corner with a small canvas covered in slashes of paint. The strokes seem haphazard, and I don't try to pretend to understand what I'm looking at. Mira's laptop sits open on two textbooks, the screen black and reflecting my face back at me. Posters of bands I know Ramsey got her into hang on the wall across from her closet. A shaggy carmine circle rug takes up the center of the floor, black slippers tossed on it. A long mirror hangs on the wall, some Polaroids and faded pictures taped to the edges. I recognize them from the ones she had in her room as a kid, but the Polaroids are new, Autumn and Bentley featured in most of them. A corkboard hangs beside the mirror. Rainbow colored pins stick sketches, ticket stubs, and random postcards into it. I walk over and study some of the tickets before focusing on the postcards.

"Your dad sent these?" I point to one of the Eiffel Tower, looking back at Mira.

She sits on the edge of her bed, a fuzzy pillow clutched in her lap as she feathers her fingers through it. She nods, watching me. "He started sending them again a week after I got here."

Conrad sent his kids postcards from the different places he traveled to when Ramsey and Mira were kids. I remember Ramsey having a stack of them in his closet, always out of sight. Mira always stuck them on the walls in her room. I should ask Ramsey if he's getting them again too.

I nod, turning away. "It looks like you," I say, gesturing around the room.

Mira smiles, sighing.

I chuckle. "Were you nervous for me to see it?" I put my hands in my pockets and lean back against the wall.

She shrugs.

"Your room at home was always April influenced. There were touches of you in it, but this," I gesture around again. "This is all you."

She laughs. "Just wait till I actually get my own space and can paint or design it more."

I grin, picturing reds and blacks all over a house she gets full reign over. The image warms my chest, and something slithers in my gut again. I look away, finding the corner of a sketchbook sticking out on the stack of stuff atop her desk. I walk over and wiggle it free, holding it up toward her with a quirked eyebrow.

She nods and I sit down next to her and pull back the cover, looking over each page carefully. Some are filled with just hands or feet all from different angles and in different positions. But in between those, there are some pictures. A sketch of the façade of her parents' house. Autumn's face as she laughs. Ramsey sitting upside down on a couch, his curls falling toward the floor. I start to turn the page to the next sketch, glimpsing a torso before Mira's hand slams down on the page.

I look over at her, smirking. She pulls the sketchbook from me, closing it and tossing it on the table beside her bed. "Something I can't see?" I muse.

Mira hums before shoving her pillow away and throwing a leg over my lap to settle astride me. My hands land on her waist, and blood leaves my brain as she rubs against me. She stares down at me with a spark in her eyes.

"Did you just come up here to look around?" she taunts.

I surge forward, sucking her lip into my mouth and biting it. She flinches under my hands, and I skirt them down to grip her ass as she starts rocking against my quickly hardening cock. Her hands go to the back of my head, releasing my hair from the tie that holds it back and I feel it fall forward as I kiss her. My tongue finds hers and she pulls herself closer, making her chest squish against mine, while her fingers tighten in my hair. She pulls it a bit and I groan into her mouth.

I fall back on the bed, taking Mira with me before rolling. Her legs stay wrapped around my hips as I pull back to hover over her, feet still on the ground. I smile at her dazed look and reddened lips.

"Beautiful," I murmur, and her eyes widen.

Unbuttoning her jeans, I pull them down her legs, kissing just below the hem of her shirt where it lays rumpled across her stomach. Her breath heaves as I bunch her shirt up over her chest and continue to pepper kisses across her torso. When I get to the edge of her bra, I pull back, tugging her shirt over her head. Once she lays in her underwear, I take her hands in mine, interlocking our fingers. She tends to put her arms around herself at this point and I hate it when she tries to hide from me. I hold her hands above her head, dipping down to kiss and nip at her throat. A whine escapes her throat as she wiggles beneath me, but I pin her hips to the bed with my own, pressing myself into her for some friction.

"Harley," she whimpers. She always gives up control to me at first, but I love making her so impatient she tries to take it back. Her hands tighten around mine and I press them a little more firmly into her mattress as she tries to pull them away. I tsk against her throat before venturing down and swirling my tongue across the tops of her breasts above the edge of her bra. She pulls at my hands again and I sit up.

"Did you need something, Meerkat?" I ask, breath coming out hard.

She pants as well, but determination shines in her eyes as she tries to buck me off. "Too many clothes," she says when the attempt is unsuccessful.

I smile. "Yes, I think you are in too many clothes." I gather her hands into one of mine before reaching down to unhook her bra with the front clasp she prefers. She huffs, rolling her hips and I hiss when the move presses against my dick.

"Problem?" she asks with a smirk.

I pull her bra cups to the side, her breasts spilling out

and shake my head. "No problem here," I say as I dive down to suck her left nipple into my mouth. Her back arches and she cries out when I pull it hard between my teeth. I watch her face as she closes her eyes and breathes, forgetting to fight me. I grind my hips into her as I repeat my actions on her right nipple before lapping over it with the tip of my tongue. Her jaw clenches and she pulls air in between her teeth.

I release her hands, grabbing the back of my shirt and tugging it over my head. Her palms press into my chest once bare and I close my eyes, reveling in their warmth for a moment. She pops the button of my jeans, leaning up in a sitting position as I stand before her. Her tongue drags along the curve of my hip bone as she shuffles my jeans and boxers down together. I kick them away and she grips my cock, making my spine snap straight. Her tongue leaves my skin and then her lips wrap around my tip. I stare down at her, hands fisted at my side. I have only fucked her mouth that one time in the forest, the memory haunting me every time I jack off in the shower. Mira looks up at me, a smirk on her lips as she rolls her tongue down the underside of my dick.

I hiss, gritting my teeth. "Don't tease."

Mira pulls her head back. "You're one to talk." She lunges forward and sucks me down her throat. I groan and my head falls back as all thoughts leave my brain and the feeling of being in her warm wet mouth overwhelms me. She grips the sides of my hips as she quickly bobs.

I let her work me for a minute before I feel a tingle at the base of my spine and look down. "Mira," I call, but she ignores me. "Mira," I try again more forcefully but she just picks up her pace, eyes closed. I grab the back of her head, pulling her off me and her eyes fly open.

"I'm not finishing in your mouth tonight," I growl before grabbing her waist and tossing her further up the bed. I watch her breasts jiggle as she lands, my cock twitching at the sight, before I follow. I pull her underwear off and throw them behind us, laying over her so our skin meets almost everywhere. Her hands cup my face, and she pulls my mouth to hers. My tongue explores the taste of me on her. I slide my hand down her stomach to her wet center and part her lips with my thumb. Damp thighs grip my hand as I sink a finger into her, finding no resistance.

I moan with Mira, using my other hand to push her thighs open as I work her further. Her eyes slam closed when I push another finger in, rocking her hips with me. I massage the inside of her thigh as I hold one of her legs down flat to the mattress. Her hands slide down my back, gripping and scratching over my shoulders. I kiss her jaw, picking up the pace of my hand as her mouth falls open in a perfect O. I know exactly where to press inside her at this angle and hit that spot repeatedly as my thumb rubs over her clit in circles. She tenses, then cries out, as her inner muscles grip my fingers, and she digs her nails into me.

I love watching her when she comes.

I move my hand lazily, continuing to help her ride the high at a slower pace.

Kissing my way to her ear, she jumps when I bite her earlobe and I smile when her hand comes up to pull my hair and move my head back. Our eyes meet and her mouth spreads into a languid smile. I pull my hand from her center, still rubbing and massaging her inner thigh with my other. Licking her off me, she releases my hair to pull my fingers from my mouth before wrapping her own lips around them and sucking.

My hips jut into her stomach, dick rubbing against her

as I watch her savor herself. I groan. She smiles when she releases them, pulling my head back down to kiss me long and hard. I let her lead, her other hand leaving my back and sliding between us to grip my cock. She rubs me a few times, still moving her tongue slowly with mine before pulling away from my mouth and rubbing the tip of my dick up and down her wet center. I shudder and watch her face as she watches mine. Mira notches my cock at her entrance. My breath hitches as her muscles pull around my tip and I thrust forward, sliding into her quickly. Bottoming out, I stop, staring down at her as she grins up at me.

"Fuck me, Harley." She's all breath. I pull both her thighs wider, flattening them against the mattress as I pull back and thrust in hard. She grunts as I repeat the movement, eyes closing and hands feathering back into my hair. I watch her as I pump my hips, ecstasy pulling at her gorgeous features. I lean down and kiss the center of her throat. Chasing our highs, I bite the crook of her neck, making her scream when she comes around me, gripping my dick inside her and making me come while my teeth still indent her skin. I push into her a few more times, releasing my jaw and licking the red indents I left behind.

My tongue itches to say something I know I can't, so I nestle into the space between her neck and shoulder as we fall still together.

She runs her hands over my hair, quiet settling over our sweaty bodies. I let a few minutes pass, letting my heart rate lower and breathing even out before I pull back, eyes finding hers. They are bright and a little unfocused as she stares up at me. I peck her lips before untangling us and pulling out.

I watch my cum leak out her, entranced by the sight before a spike of panic shoots through me.

"Fuck!"

"What?" Mira sits up quickly, looking around.

"I forgot a condom." I run my hands through my hair, an image of Mira pregnant flashing behind my eyes. My fear increases when the image makes my chest warm, but the anger on imaginary Mira's face guts me.

Real Mira sighs and falls back on the bed. "I'm back on the pill. As long as you're clean, we're good." She stretches her arms over her head, and I watch her.

"I'm clean," I whisper and the image of pregnant Mira floats away. I ignore the feeling in my chest at the idea fading.

Mira nods, and I hold my hand out.

"Shower?"

She smiles, taking my hand and letting me pull her up. She pokes her head out the door, looking both ways before pulling me quickly to her bathroom.

I laugh. "Coast clear?"

She rolls her eyes, reaching in to turn the shower on. "Shut up. I don't want to get caught."

I lean back against her sink as we wait for the water to heat. Her words roll around my brain. I shouldn't want to get caught either. But the fear of it leaves me half the time when I'm with her. The idea of Ramsey knowing about us makes my blood run cold, but Mira tends to make me feel too warm to notice.

18

After Harley pulls me into the shower and eats me out again, I can't stand properly. He finds it hilarious and picks me up, situating my legs around his waist as he laughs.

"Don't worry. I'll carry you, Meerkat," he whispers as he walks back to my room. We fall onto my bed, staying wrapped up in each other as he pulls the duvet over our bodies.

My eyes flutter closed. "Are you staying?"

He kisses my forehead, lips soft against my skin. "No, I should go before Janette gets back." My grip on him tightens and he laughs. "Don't worry, we still have some time."

I open my eyes, studying his face. He has a scar the side of his nose from falling off his bike when we were kids. I rub my thumb against it.

"Why didn't you let me see the next sketch?" he asks. I keep my eyes on my thumb, avoiding his as I feel them searching my face. "You never cared when I looked at them before."

I chuckle. "Ramsey always showed them to you before. You never sought them out." I glance up, meeting his eyes.

"I'm seeking now." I roll my eyes, biting my lip. I don't want him to see the sketches of him I've been working on. Not only are they unfinished, but we're short term. Drawing him reveals how deep my feelings run and I don't want him to think I can't handle just being fuck buddies.

This will never be anything more.

"Are you drawing porn?" Harley smirks.

I scoff, rolling my eyes. "No, Harley, I'm not drawing porn."

"Well, now I'm much more interested." He sits up and reaches over my head to grab the sketchbook. I grab at his arm, trying to stop him, but he simply holds it out of my reach as I stretch.

He chuckles before flipping us and straddling my waist, pinning one of my arms to my side with his thighs. I use my other hand to try to grab the book from him, but he pins my hand down easily, smiling over me.

Setting the book down beside my head, he flips it open one handed. He squeezes the hand he has pinned down before speeding past the first few pages he already saw and stopping at the page I stopped him from seeing before. He freezes, eyes roving the page and I squirm underneath him, freeing my other arm and throwing my hands up to cover my face. My cheeks flame under my palms and I imagine myself disappearing completely.

I hear Harley close the book and put it back on the side table, my heart lurching as I picture him walking out and going back to ignoring me forever. His fingers wrap around my wrists and tug my hands away from my face. My eyes meet his and the reverence there floors me.

"You need to change majors. You are way too talented to waste your time doing something you don't enjoy."

I bite my lip, looking away from his face. My eyes find the postcards pinned to my corkboard across the room and I stare at them. My eyes lose focus the longer the silence stretches on.

Harley sighs, leaning down and kissing my mouth before kissing my cheek and rolling to the side. He gathers me up against his chest so that we are spooning. He loves cuddling after sex, always taking a few moments to hold me like this whenever we fuck. I stare forward with unfocused eyes.

"You're allowed to do things for yourself, Mira," Harley whispers. "You don't have to always try to keep your parents happy."

I close my eyes, the backs of them itching, and swallow. Turning around in his arms, I kiss him in response. He settles me under his chin after, and I sigh before falling asleep.

I wake up to Harley swearing. Sunlight streams in through the thin pink curtains hanging over my window and I rub my eyes as he quickly untangles his limbs from mine. Once he is free, he jumps from the bed, making me hiss at the cold air invading my blanket cocoon.

"What's wrong?" I grumble, snuggling back into the bed's warmth when I see it's only seven on my alarm clock.

"I fell asleep. I didn't mean to stay the night. Ramsey's going to question where I went if I don't get back."

I sit up, letting the comforter fall to my waist, and stretch. Harley has his jeans pulled up and pauses while buttoning them to stare at me.

"Shirt, Harley." I get out of bed and grab my fuzzy robe off my desk chair. Wrapping it around myself, I walk out into the living room. Janette's door is still slightly ajar, looking the same as it did last night and I knock, calling her name. When no one responds, I push it open, finding her room empty, bed made. I walk over to the kitchen, but the dorm is empty. I stroll back to my room, finding Harley dressed and pulling on his socks.

"Janette never came home last night, so you're in the clear." I lean my hip against my door frame, and he nods, standing up and walking over to me.

He puts his hands on my shoulders as I cross my arms over my chest. Leaning down, he kisses my cheek. "I'll text you," he says and then walks to the front door to pull on his shoes.

I watch, thinking about how nice it was to sleep with him, even if waking up was abrupt.

He throws me a smile before disappearing and I frown when the door closes behind him. It feels like a hook lodges into my sternum and I rub at it for a minute before the door opens again and Janette walks in.

She freezes when she sees me, still in the same sweater and jeans from the bar last night. I quirk an eyebrow as she sheepishly breaks eye contact and starts pulling off her boots.

"Have a good night?" I ask.

She gives me an *mmhmm* before walking toward the kitchen and starting the Keurig. I walk over too.

"Saw that guy who came with your brother in the hallway," she murmurs.

My blood freezes and I try to school my reaction.

She glances over as she reaches into the cabinet for a k-cup. "Don't worry, I won't say anything. Don't even know how I'd get in touch with your brother." She chuckles as she loads the Keurig and grabs a mug. "He's hot."

My forehead furrows as I bob my head in response. Janette hasn't been as cold to me the last week and when Layla brought her along last night, she fit in pretty seamlessly, not saying anything passive aggressive. I don't know what started this new version of her, but I also didn't see Christopher's car in the lot last weekend.

"You break things off with Christopher before you spent the night somewhere else?" It comes out harsher than I mean it, but I don't know how to have a conversation with Janette without it feeling like a minefield.

Janette nods, avoiding my eyes. "Yeah, I'm seeing someone else now." Her voice wobbles a little and I feel a bit bad for pushing her.

"Good for you," I say genuinely, before heading to my room to get ready. After throwing on a comfy sweatshirt and jeans, I head past Janette, now sipping her drink on the couch, and put on my shoes. The tension in the room seems different, almost awkward now instead of unfriendly. I nod to her, and she nods back before I grab my keys and leave.

Axel opens the door when I knock on Bentley's suite, just in a tee shirt and boxers. He lets me in, scratching the back of his head and yawning. "He's in the shower."

I nod, my gut twisting as I realize I never texted to make sure Bentley made it back okay.

Axel disappears into his room, and I sit on the leather couch, pulling my phone out and checking social media as I wait. Bentley emerges from the bathroom in just a towel a few minutes later.

"Mira," he says, jumping a bit when he sees me. "Fuck, sorry I didn't think you'd be here this early. I just need a minute to get dressed and then we can head out."

I wave him off. "I woke up early so you're good. Take your time, no rush."

He walks into his bedroom, and I scroll through pictures online. I get a notification that someone followed me, and I click to open it, finding Harley's username and profile. I wasn't allowed to have social media until I was sixteen and when I finally made profiles, he never followed me back or accepted my follow request. I scroll through his private page for a minute before closing the app and pulling up our texts.

> Finally following me back I see.

The little texting bubbles appear instantly.

HARLEY

> Figured it's the least I could do after you sucked my dick last night.

My stomach clenches at the memory. The hook twists a bit more as I remember him fleeing my dorm this morning.

I close the texts, leaving him on read, and go back to scrolling through his photos. A lot of them are in the gym or promoting membership deals or classes, but a few have the Ravens or are throwbacks of him in his football uniform. Not a single girl appears on his page, and I let myself smile at that.

"Ready?" Bentley asks, coming back out of his room dressed.

I nod and we walk over to the campus café, ordering our usual drinks. Bentley carries them over to one of the few free tables in the corner.

"So, what happened with Harley after you left?" He sips his coffee, and I wrap both my hands around my hot chocolate.

"Guess I'm going first," I mumble, and Bentley smiles, fear flashing in his eyes. I table my curiosity for later. "Do me a favor? Don't say anything until I'm done." He nods, and I take a deep breath. "I've been hooking up with Harley the last few weeks." Bentley keeps his mouth closed, but his eyes widen a bit and I scramble to explain. "It's just a friends with benefits thing that we started a little bit after he started training me. I got followed home from the birthday party at the Ravens' place and I wanted to learn how to defend myself after. I accidentally ended up at his gym and he offered to train me personally when one of his trainers started hitting on me. We started hooking up a bit after that because it became too hard to be around each other and not have little mishaps after the kissing incidents."

Bentley looks away from me and sips his coffee. "I wanted to tell you so badly, but you didn't want me being around him anymore after that day at the gym. It was hard though. He came by and apologized, and we started this whole thing. I know it's not going to end well but I can deal with the fallout when that comes. I haven't been able to start anything serious with anyone else so might as well try purging him from my system while I have the opportunity."

I wait, sipping my drink so that I don't keep rambling. Bentley just watches people move around the room, turning to look at me again a moment later. His face stays neutral, and panic claws at my insides. "Say something, Bent."

He sighs. "I'm not mad you didn't tell me. I get why you didn't. But, Mir, I don't think it's healthy." He leans forward, elbows on the table. "You're not just hiding from me, you're hiding from Ramsey and he's going to find out eventually. And when that happens, Harley will pull back again, the way he did after your fifteenth."

"I know," I say, leaning back and sighing. "I know this ends badly, Bent. I'm preparing for that. Harley doesn't want anything more and I have killed any hope that he will." The lie slips out my mouth easily as a little seed of hope wiggles in my chest.

"He won't choose you over Ramsey, Mir." The words stab me, but I've thought them to myself before, the wound they create already open inside me.

"I know," I whisper.

"And his friendship with Ramsey will be ruined."

I sit up. "We would end it before that could happen."

Bentley shakes his head. "You might not have a say in that, Mir. What if he finds out?"

I grit my teeth. "He won't find out, Bentley." Bentley holds up his hands in surrender.

"Okay, let's say he doesn't. This can't go on forever. It's going to end with him hurting you, Mira." Bentley reaches across the table and grabs one of my hands. He squeezes it. "It doesn't end any other way."

"I know that." I squeeze his hand back. "And when it does, I'll be able to mourn and move on. I couldn't do that before, Bentley. I don't know why but I couldn't. When this ends, I'll finally have closure."

"Closure?" Bentley mulls the idea over. I nod and he sighs, taking his hand back to drink again. "Are you at least exclusive? Herpes is forever, Amiria."

I snort then think it over. "I don't know," I whisper, looking down at the table. We never established if this was an exclusive thing. Harley said he was clean last night, but that doesn't necessarily mean he isn't fucking other people. I twist my hands together. I glance up and Bentley looks back at me, sympathy in his eyes.

"I'll be there when it ends, Mir. You know that right?" Tears prick the back of my eyes for the second time in twenty-four hours and I blink them back.

"I know, Bent. I'm sorry for not telling you earlier." He

nods once and I take another sip of my now cold chocolate. "Harley thinks I should change my major." Bentley's eyebrows rise. "He saw my sketchbook last night and thinks I should switch to art."

"He's not wrong. I never got why you wanted to do chem." He plays with the lid of his cup.

I sigh. "My dad suggested it. Thought it would be good for me to go into science and chemistry was my best one at Emerald Grove."

Bentley quirks an eyebrow. "I mean sure a B- is better than a C," he muses.

I roll my eyes. "My mom overheard, and they started to fight about him trying to influence my choices and I didn't want them to fight so I just told my mom I thought it was a good idea." I shrug, looking down at my drink and twisting the satin scrunchie on my wrist. When I finally glance up at Bentley, his mouth hangs agape.

"Amiria Nicole Adams, you did not choose a college major to stop your parents from fighting."

I shrug again, moving my eyes off him to look at the room. "I don't not like chemistry."

"Once more, with feeling, Mir."

I look back at him. "I don't want my mom to get upset and if I switch, she'll know I was unhappy and blame my dad again. Ramsey and I aren't there to keep the peace anymore, Bent. I don't want to be the reason they're fighting."

"That's convoluted. April will be happy that you are happy and if you think she can't tell that you're not right now, you don't give her enough credit." He takes a long pull of his coffee. "And Ramsey never worried about keeping the peace with your parents. That was the burden you took on, Mir. And their relationship is not on your shoulders."

I hear the words, and he isn't the first person to say them to me. Harley and Ramsey have tried to get me to see that all throughout our childhoods. But the idea of doing something for myself, that I know will hurt my mother, feels selfish. Chemistry isn't that bad.

Dad's postcards flash in my head.

"You should switch, Mir," Bentley says determinedly. "Not just because you don't like chem, but you're an amazing artist. You deserve the chance to dive into that more."

I nod, plastering a smile on my face. "What was it you wanted to tell me about?" I ask.

Bentley swallows without taking a sip of his drink and looks me in the eye. We hold eye contact for a few moments before he shakes his head fractionally. "Doesn't seem so serious now. I just hooked up with this girl last night and she was awful so now I'm worried about seeing her in class later."

I stare at him skeptically. He seemed more concerned about telling me all about it when we walked over here.

"Seriously, I can go into detail if you want." He waggles his eyebrows, and I scrunch up my nose.

"No thanks." I hold up my hands, looking down at the table for a second. He sips his drink and starts to tell me how he isn't sure what to say if she wants to see him again and we laugh. He comes up with some jokes he can use to deflect and I lean into the conversation, ignoring the niggling feeling that he's holding something back.

19

amsey picks me up outside of West Tower the Wednesday morning before Thanksgiving. Harley sits in the passenger seat of his Jeep, smiling at me as I round the hood. The last time I saw him, he fucked me slowly against the closed door to his office while Cheryl opened the gym. His hand stayed against my mouth the whole time and I came so hard, he had to hold me up afterward.

Then he cupped my face and groaned about how being in the same house with me and Ramsey for the long weekend is going to be torture. I just pecked him quick and said we'd need to find a way to alleviate the problem.

Now as Ramsey loads my duffel into his trunk, I'm starting to realize I may have underestimated the torture factor. I just want to spend the car ride home touching Harley.

"What the fuck did you pack in this?" I close the door and lean over the backseat to look at Ramsey.

"Bricks, just to piss you off. Lugging it down here was a bitch." Harley snorts and I twist to face forward, smiling at the back of his head before sliding over so I can see his profile from the back. I buckle myself in and Ramsey slams the trunk, coming back around to the front.

"Hope you didn't forget anything. I am not turning back around." He pulls away from the curb, leaving campus and starting the trek home. The first hour consists of Ramsey and I talking about classes and how busy it's been lately now that the snow has made going off campus harder for everyone without cars. Harley notes that membership cancellations have gone up now that it's colder but that's typical for them. He smiles back at me a few times, and I watch Ramsey, noting he doesn't seem to notice the change in his best friend's demeanor around me.

"This ride was a lot better in a limo," I grumble when Ramsey rolls over a pothole and the whole car jumps.

"Should have asked Marshall to send one for you then." Ramsey drums along to a song on the steering wheel.

I roll my eyes and Harley looks out his window. "He probably would have if I did."

Harley's hand tightens into a fist on his lap.

I smirk, wondering how far I can push him. "Might call him when we get there and see if he can arrange for one back."

Harley's jaw clenches.

I lean forward, head between the front seats and sneer at my brother while watching Harley's reaction. "And you'll have to drive back all by yourselves."

"Would be a lot quieter of a ride," Harley grumbles, and I fall back in my seat, heart beating wildly. Ramsey laughs and Harley glances back at me, eyes wide before he schools his face and faces forward again.

I look out the window, biting my tongue. I pushed him but seeing the Harley from just a few months ago bite back startled me. It was stupid of me to think I'd get any other reaction with Ramsey in the car. I spend the rest of the ride dodging their attempts to pull me into more conversation, feeling Harley turn over his shoulder to glance at me a few times. I mull over the incident, knowing he didn't mean it, but him doing that makes me realize how much it will actually hurt when things between us end. And it wasn't even pain that I felt, it was a numb emptiness that I never considered. Will losing him completely this time make me feel empty?

I'm still thinking about everything when we pull up to the house, Ramsey parking crooked in the driveway. Mom comes running down the stairs again, grabbing Harley first because his side is closest this time. Ramsey and I go to the truck to get our bags.

"You okay?" he whispers as he passes me my duffel.

I nod and throw on a smile. "Fine." He grabs Harley's bag since he is still trapped by his door with our mother.

"You were just quiet there after a while." I nod, and he grabs my arm before I can walk away. "Was it what Harley said? Because he didn't mean it, just doesn't seem to like Marshall much lately." I furrow my brow and he chuckles. "I've noticed him glaring at him a few times. I don't know what happened with them, but you fawning over Marshall being able to get you a limo seemed to piss him off."

Mom comes around the car and grabs Ramsey in a hug. Harley walks over behind her to take the bags Ramsey dropped hugging her back. I watch, a bit frozen, coming to terms with my brother not being so oblivious to everything as I thought.

Once she releases Ramsey, she engulfs me, kissing the side of my head and squeezing me tight. I squeeze back, closing my eyes before opening them to find Harley staring at us with a fond smile. Ramsey heads inside, bag in hand. I let go of Mom and she pulls back, leaving one arm over my shoulders as we walk in together. Harley trails behind us.

"I'm so glad I have my three kids back home with me. It's been quiet in this place without you lot." We break apart to walk through the door and I stop in the threshold, almost bumping into Ramsey.

"Dad?" I whisper before breaking into a smile and moving around my frozen brother to run up to my father. He hugs me when I reach him, the hug a bit stiffer than Mom's.

"How's school been, Amiria?" he asks when we pull apart and I grimace.

"Good." I nod and Dad nods back, looking over my head. "And you two?"

"Harley's not in school, Dad," Ramsey answers, folding his arms over his chest.

Mom squeezes around him, putting a hand on his shoulder. Dad's eyes burn into her fingers, and I note the lack of wedding ring once again.

"You're doing good though, right, Ramsey?" she asks.

He nods, not looking down at her.

"Good," Dad murmurs, squeezing my shoulder. "Can I talk to you two in my office?" He nods to the boys. Harley glances down at me before nodding and following Ramsey and Dad down the hall. Mom watches them go, worrying her bottom lip before she clears her face and turns back to me.

"Want to help me make brownies?" She raises an eyebrow and I smile, following her into the kitchen. She starts pulling out the ingredients she needs, and I sit at one of the stools on one side of the island. Helping Mom make anything pretty much just means keeping her company while she does it all herself.

"So how are your classes really going?" she asks when she has everything on the island and starts pulling out bowls and measuring cups from the island drawers.

"They're fine, Mom," I say, leaning over to steal a few chocolate chips from the half empty bag. She swats my hand with a spoon, and I pull it back and pout. She gives me a look and I sigh. "It's just a bit harder that I thought it would be." I shrug.

She nods, starting to measure the wet ingredients out. "I saw your midterm grades. You're doing really well in your art class." She smiles as she pours the oil into the mixing bowl.

I blanche. "You saw my midterms?"

She looks up and nods slowly. "I have a parent account that's tied to your and Ramsey's student ones so I can pay your tuition online and see your grades."

I chew my bottom lip. "I could have done better in my main classes." I pull at my scrunchie, not glancing up.

She starts cracking eggs and hums. "Well, I'm sure it's hard to do well when you don't like your classes." I look up and Mom glances over at me with her head still tilted down. "I know you, Mira. I know you don't want to be studying chemistry." I open my mouth to argue but she holds her hand up. "It's okay, we don't have to argue about this now. We can talk more after dinner." She gives me a tight-lipped smile and my brows pull together as she goes back to adding vanilla to the bowl. "Any new boys in your life?" Her voice lilts as she asks me the question and she peeks up, catching me rolling my eyes. "Or girls?"

"No, Mom." I glance back over my shoulder to where Ramsey and Harley disappeared with Dad. "Is Dad home for the whole weekend?" I turn back as she starts pouring sugar into the bowl with the wet ingredients.

"You'll have to ask him." She doesn't glance up and I nod. Her posture has stiffened, and I don't know what exactly agitated her.

"I'm going to go see what the boys are doing," I whisper, and she nods, smiling at me as I get off the stool. I head upstairs, using the small staircase off the kitchen and wander the hall, seeing the game room door open and hearing simulated shooting.

They sit on either end of the couch across from the TV, mashing buttons on the controllers in their laps. I walk in and plop down on the armchair off to the side, throwing my legs over the arm.

Ramsey glances over at me before looking back at the TV. "Mom baking?"

I mumble *mmhmm* and pull out my phone before saying, "Brownies."

Harley nods, eyes never leaving the screen. I scroll mindlessly on the internet for a few minutes before he asks, "Marshall not home for the holiday?" I glance over at him. Ramsey does the same and then shakes his head slightly at me.

"No, his parents took him to go skiing in the Alps," I say, watching Harley who doesn't seem to react at all. Ramsey pulls his controller up closer to his chest, fingers straining to move faster. "Autumn went home with Aria to avoid seeing her parents." Ramsey's jaw tightens and Harley glances over at him. "Guess you two are stuck with me for the next few days." I watch them play over the top of my phone, neither looking over at me or saying anything more.

A few minutes later, Ramsey pauses the game, muttering about going pee before leaving the room. My chin rests in my hand as I scroll through some random person's profile who sent me a friend request.

"You shouldn't poke your brother," Harley mumbles, thumbing over his own phone screen.

I peer over at him, brows furrowing. I shrug when his head lifts up and his eyes flash.

His tone hardens. "I'm serious, Amiria. Don't push him right now."

Anger strikes me, remembering the words he said in the car. "I'll push Ramsey all I want. You don't get to tell me what to do. He's the reason we have to sneak around like some dirty little secret."

Harley rears back, eyes wide at my words. I instantly regret saying them and chew the inside of my cheek as I zone out staring at the TV.

"It's not Ramsey's fault we have to sneak around, Mir," Harley whispers. "*I'm* the one who doesn't want him finding out."

I nod, still not looking back at him or focusing my vision. "I know." My voice sounds flat even in my ears.

I see Harley turn back toward me in my peripheral. "Maybe we should stop if you're starting to resent him." The words come out quiet but strong, no cracks or wobbles like mine would have if I tried to suggest we end things. It's almost casual, and cold creeps into my veins.

Ramsey walks back in and plops down, wordlessly starting their game back up. I can see shapes moving on the screen and hear everything around me, but I sit through two more games before I finally feel like I can move and get up, leaving them both behind without a second glance.

I wind up lying on my bed on top of the comforter, staring up at my ceiling while my mind swirls. I hug a pillow to my chest, wishing I could call Bentley to talk about anything else other than the thoughts bouncing around in my head. If I call Autumn, she'll know something's weird, and I haven't told her about Harley and me yet. I didn't even get the chance to ask the boys what Dad wants to talk to them about in his office.

Do I resent Ramsey for only being able to have a friends-with-benefits relationship with Harley?

The same question keeps blaring intermittently when I try to think about literally anything else. Harley's voice as he suggested we end things plays on repeat in the background. I can see the feelings in his eyes, in the little things he does for me when we are together, but he suggested we end things so easily. And the worst part is his reasoning. He doesn't want to come between my brother and me, the same way I would give him up so I don't come between my brother and *him*.

I squeeze the pillow tighter.

If Ramsey is close to figuring things out, can I step away and lose Harley for him?

The resounding *no* in my head makes my heart pound. I don't resent Ramsey. He'll get over it if he finds out about us. I suddenly know he would.

I resent *Harley*. I resent him not being able to risk Ramsey being mad for a little bit to choose me.

I sit up, still clutching the pillow. That's unfair. Ramsey's his best friend, his family. And he's not just risking losing my brother. He spends every holiday with my family. If he's scared of losing Ramsey, he's scared of losing us all. If I had to choose between losing my family or losing Harley, I wouldn't make that decision. But that won't happen. Ramsey would never cut either of us off over this, even if he was livid at the beginning. And my parents think of Harley as their other son. They won't cut him off like his parents did.

Would I put up with this for someone who put his best friend's opinion over me, if the best friend wasn't my brother? Not with the history Harley and I have. Not when I am falling in love with him as hard as I am.

My breath stutters in my throat. Fuck.

I love Harley.

That's why the idea of losing him made me feel empty in the car. That's why I can't choose between him and Ramsey. And that's why I got so mad when he tried to protect his friendship with Ramsey over his relationship with me.

My eyes start to water as I realize how this will actually end. His voice suggesting we end things in the game room plays in my ears again and again. I should have just taken Bentley's advice and shut the door in Harley's face when he showed up at Bentley's dorm at the beginning of the semester.

But I can't bring myself to regret getting to be with him.

"Mira!" Mom's voice comes up the stairs. "Dinner!"

I glance at my clock, realizing hours have passed while I spiraled in my room. I drop the pillow and stand, stretching. With a sigh, I drag my feet down the hall and stairs to the informal dining room, a little surprised to see Dad at his seat at the head of the table. Mom sits on his right, Ramsey across from her and Harley beside him. Mom dishes some lasagna onto her plate, smiling at me as I sit beside her. She reaches over and squeezes my hand on my lap, giving me a questioning look and I shake my head, taking the dish she offers. Nobody speaks as we pass things around, the sound of utensils scraping dishes ringing through the room. I avoid Harley's eyes, noticing him watching me in my peripheral and then frowning down at his plate. I sigh quietly, digging into my food and not tasting it as I slowly eat.

After half my dinner is gone and no one says anything,

Dad clears his throat, calling all of our attention to him. "Your mother and I have an announcement." Mom fidgets with her fingers in her lap, seeming to try to twist the ring that no longer sits on her finger.

"Conrad, maybe we should wait until after dinner," she chirps, smiling at the three of us.

"What's going on?" Ramsey asks slowly, eyes swiveling between them. Harley glances between them as well before his eyes widen and his head whips over to me.

"Your mother and I have decided to divorce." Dad looks Ramsey in the eye as he says it, everyone stopping all movement. Mom closes her eyes for a moment before glancing between Ramsey and me. I stare at Dad who looks over at me blankly.

"What?" I whisper, the cold from earlier seeping into my bones.

Mom grabs my hand, squeezing my numbing fingers. Harley's hand flinches toward mine before settling as he continues to watch me. "It's not your fault, sweet pea." She watches my face, worry written all over her features.

"No, it's his," Ramsey says with a tight jaw as he stares our father down. Dad looks back at him, jaw ticking.

"This was a mutual decision, Ramsey," Dad says in a measured tone.

"I'm sure it was. Mom probably wanted to finally be free of you and you can now go be even more absent from our lives than you already are." I close my eyes, feeling a foot rub against my ankle a moment later.

"Are you moving out?" I whisper, not opening my eyes.

"No one's moving out," Mom insists. "Things are going to be exactly as they have been, while we figure everything out."

I open my eyes, my brother and father still staring each other down.

"Stop acting childish, Ramsey," Dad says between his teeth. Ramsey's fists clench around his utensils and Mom slams her hand down on the table, pulling both of their attention.

I jump, immediately looking at Harley whose grey eyes meet mine. He rubs his foot against me again, seeming to physically hold himself back from reaching across the table for me.

"He is reacting, Conrad," Mom says, voice tense. "He is not being childish. This is hard for them."

Dad grunts. "Yes, I'm sure it is hard for *them*," he hisses. The two seem to spar with their eyes and I look between them, my breathing picking up.

I scoot my chair back, limbs trembling a bit as I turn and run back to my room, ignoring the two voices who call my name. I slam my door closed behind me, turning my lights off and burying myself underneath my comforter as the tears hit and everything I was numb to washes over me like a tsunami.

I pass out hours later, face a mess with snot and tears that bleed into my pillow.

20

Harley

Light from the hallway hits Mira's face when I crack her door open as slowly and quietly as possible.

The house has been silent for hours, the only light while I made my way up the stairs coming from the automatic floor lights that turned on as I moved past the motion sensors. I slinked silently from the guest room after counting down the minutes to one a.m., assuming everyone would be asleep by now.

After Mira fled the room, Ramsey and Conrad started a screaming match, April trying to break it up by verbally sparring with Conrad herself. Eventually I pulled Ramsey away, taking him back to his room and hearing Mira crying through her door as we passed. The sound pulled Ramsey out of his rage, both of us pausing and looking at each other. I wanted to go in there and hold her so much my palms itched.

"We should probably leave her to cry it out," Ramsey whispered, eyes transfixed on the door. I had to grit my teeth and force my feet to follow him as he walked away. We went to the game room at the end of hall and silently played for hours. Ramsey said nothing, only speaking up to swear when I killed him in the game. When he finally shut the game down and said he was going to sleep, I nodded, tossing my controller, and trying to figure out how I could get into Mira's room without him noticing. Not sure how to do it, I walked down to the guest room, running into April as she wiped down the kitchen. I said goodnight and she came over and hugged me, saying goodnight before patting my back and nodding to the guest wing.

I paced my room, watching the clock the rest of the time, waiting for the coast to clear.

Mira's head lies on her pillow, everything below her chin burrowed under the comforter. Her wavy hair splays behind her in a tangled mess across the bed. One of her hands lays under her cheek, her face peaceful in sleep. I turn around to close her door quietly, moonlight still lighting the room enough to see. I turn back, Mira's eyes fluttering open. She blearily watches me cross the floor to the open side of her bed.

"What are you doing?" she mumbles, voice groggy with sleep and thick from crying.

I slide into the bed, under her comforter, and scoot over to be next to her. She stares up at me, bottom lip trembling.

"Harley," she whispers. I pull her into my chest, one hand around her waist, the other one on the back of her head. I rub both spots as she starts to cry again.

"It's okay, baby," I whisper into her hair.

"I feel so stupid," she mumbles against my shirt. I pull back a little to peer down at her. Mira avoids my eyes, wiping under her own. I tug her hands away gently and replace them with my own, swiping her tears and tilting her head up to look at me.

"Why? This isn't your fault, Meerkat." She blinks, thick lashes darkening as they soak up her tears.

She sighs, settling into me more. "I wasted so much time and energy trying to stop them from fighting. I tried so hard to make them both happy because I *knew* they didn't do that for each other anymore." She hiccups. "I feel like I *failed*." Her voice cracks and I lean forward and kiss her forehead, holding my lips there for a few beats. Pulling back, I wipe my thumbs over her cheeks and stare into her eyes.

"Your parents divorcing has nothing to do with how good of a daughter you are or how much they love *you*. They are not doing this to hurt you, and this does not mean you have failed at *anything*." Tears slide down her cheeks and she blinks more, sucking everything in as she sniffles.

"I don't want to think about this anymore," she whispers, and I nod. I watch her as she runs a few fingers through her hair, snagging on some knots and pulling them apart. Her brown eyes flit back to meet mine, sparking. "Take my mind off things?" she asks, hands pulling out of her hair to reach under the duvet and tug at the hem of my tee shirt. I let her drag it off and let her kiss me once it disappears. Her mouth moves fast and insistently, hands pushing at my chest so that I roll onto my back. She follows, rolling on top of me and sliding her hands down my arms to move my hands to her waist.

I pull back. "This isn't why I came here, Mira," I whisper, looking between her eyes as she stares down at me. She rolls her hips intentionally, my grip on her tightening as the movement wakes up my dick.

"I know, Harley." She pecks my lips. "I just need to stop thinking for a few minutes," she whispers against my mouth, biting my bottom lip. I groan, pulling back again to search her face for a moment. I can't tell if this is a bad idea or if denying her will just make her more upset. And I can't get rid of the ache in my chest to comfort her.

Rolling us over, I take her face in my hands. "Okay, I'll take your mind off it." She smiles as my hips align with hers and we grind against each other, my tongue sliding into her waiting mouth. She moans and I pull back, both of our head turning toward the door.

"You need to be quiet."

She nods, eyes wide and licks her lips. "No teasing this time, Har. I just need you inside me."

I shake my head, cock fully hardened at her words and brain malfunctioning from the blood loss. "I won't hurt you, Meerkat." My hand snakes down her clothed stomach, dipping into her underwear and parting her thighs. Her skin is already damp, but not nearly enough for her to take me without some stretching.

"I need a little pain right now. Please." I groan at her words, forehead falling onto her shoulder. She runs a hand through my hair and whispers, "Please."

I sit up, ripping her shirt over her head and tearing her underwear off. She bites her bottom lip while I pull off my boxers and lay back down over her.

"You need to be quiet," I repeat, placing my palm over her mouth. Her lips part, breath fanning against my hand while she pants. My other hand dips back between her legs, and I thrust two fingers into her, pumping quickly to try to get her ready faster. I roll my thumb over her clit and bite one of her nipples, playing my cards quickly as she arches off the bed beneath me, her cry muffled by my hand. Biting the other nipple too, I rub her a bit more rapidly and her hand grips my shoulder, the other reaching down to run over my cock. I swear into her chest when she slowly pumps me a few times before narrowing her eyes when I surge up. I remove her hand and my own, aligning us. She stares up at me as I watch her face, slowly pushing into her. The resistance is there, the glide less smooth than any other time I've sunk into her, but her eyes seem alight when she whines beneath my hand.

I stop, only halfway there, and pull my hand away from her mouth. "You okay?"

She nods, mouth open as she huffs. "Yes, keep going."

I nod, putting my hand back over her mouth and sliding the rest of the way inside her. She sighs when our hips meet, legs coming up to wrap around me and digging her heels into my ass. Her hands come up to hold my head above her, eyes locking while I slowly pull out and slide back in. The resistance lessens. I stare down at her, breathing harshly as we move together, her hips coming up to meet mine with each thrust and hear the little groans that my hand holds back from anyone else's ears. We slide against each other, careful of the pace so as not to make the bed squeak and slowly the feeling builds up. It starts in my chest, expanding through my stomach and out to each of my limbs. I see it swimming in her eyes as her thighs start to tighten on my hips, and my tongue itches to say something.

Before I blurt out whatever it is, her head tips back, and her hips start meeting mine faster and faster. I keep up with the pace change, slamming into her and making the bed creak a bit, though the noise is faint over the blood pounding in my ears.

I reach down and lightly swipe over her clit, barely grazing it and hearing her cry underneath my hand. Her eyes squeeze shut, and she tightens all around me, coaxing me to spill inside her as I watch her come undone beneath me. We move against each other for a few more beats, riding out the high, before her eyes open and her head tips back down. Molten brown orbs swim with tears, and I quickly release her, pulling out and rushing to her bathroom. I grab two washcloths, running one under the warm water quick before running back to her and pulling the comforter away. I clean her up with the damp cloth before using the other to dab at the tears on her cheeks. She watches me, chin trembling as she clenches her jaw to keep from sobbing out.

"I'm sorry," I whisper, tossing the cloths and cradling her head in my hands.

"No," she chokes out. "It's not you. I just got overwhelmed."

I nod, staring down at her. "We shouldn't have done that."

"I don't regret it." She pulls me down so that I settle beside her again. I reach over and cover us with the duvet, wrapping my arms around her and pulling her against me. "Thank you, Harley." I look down at her. "Not just for that, but for coming in here. For being here with me."

"I wanted to come sooner," I whisper, and she sniffles, shoulders trembling. I tuck her head under my chin again, squeezing her against me.

"You should go back to the guest room," she murmurs, already falling asleep. "Someone might see you here if you fall asleep."

I kiss the top of her head. "I'll sneak out in the morning. I'm not leaving you alone tonight." I feel her arms snake around my waist, gripping me tightly as I close my eyes and revel in holding her.

21

I wake up to Harley's lips pressing against my forehead. I hum, smiling before everything from yesterday floods in and I frown.

"It's about an hour till everyone else gets up," Harley murmurs, kissing lightly down to my cheek. "I'll see you at breakfast." He kisses my lips, and I kiss him back, opening my eyes to watch him carefully climb out of bed and search the floor for his shirt and boxers.

Tucking my hands under my head I watch him dress, smiling when he glances back at me before pulling my door open, looking both ways down the hallway, and then slinking out. I chuckle at little picturing him edging along the walls like a spy through my house.

I sleep a bit more, waking alone and stretching. I stare at my ceiling, remembering when I laid in this same position yesterday and my realizations about Harley and Ramsey. I scrunch my brow, now even more confused about things after Harley stayed and held me all night. He said he wanted to end things.

Was this just pity because he saw how much my parents' announcement affected me?

My heart squelches in my chest at the thought, but then I remember staring into his eyes while we were together last night. There wasn't pity in them then. That wasn't the look of someone who only cares about me as a fuck buddy.

I sigh, getting out of bed and shaking my head. What I wouldn't give to be able to shut my brain up for a few days. I shower and get dressed, stopping myself from thinking any more about anything other than the tasks at hand.

Leaving my bedroom, I find Mom setting the last of a breakfast feast down on the table, Ramsey already seated to the right of Dad's empty chair. He sips from a glass of orange juice and raises an eyebrow at me over the rim of the glass. I wave him off, sitting down beside Mom's seat as she goes back to the kitchen and returns with salt.

"Your father left last night. He had some business in Dallas that he needed to be present for. He's going to try to make it back for dinner tonight." Mom sits down.

Harley walks in, hair still wet from a shower and fully clothed now. He walks around the table and sits down on my right, grabbing the carafe of coffee and filling a mug silently. Ramsey looks between us as I sit stock still, waiting. He merely shrugs and reaches across the table for a few slices of French toast. Mom reaches over and squeezes one of my hands before ladling some eggs onto her own plate.

Harley sips his coffee, nodding toward the food when I look over at him. "Eat," he mouths, and I turn back to the table, mechanically taking some bacon and nibbling at it.

"How'd you lot sleep?" Mom asks as we all tuck into our food.

I shrug, Harley's hand landing on my knee under the table and squeezing.

"Like a baby," Ramsey mutters, rolling his eyes. Mom winces and he apologizes, but she waves him off.

"I knew it would be hard for you guys when we told you. Just know that whatever you're feeling or any questions you have, we are both here whenever you want to talk." She looks at Ramsey then me, making sure to meet our eyes. "For all of you," she adds, staring across me to Harley. He smiles at her, taking some food onto his plate.

"I'm good right now," Ramsey says, smiling at Mom. "Kinda figured this was coming when you stopped wearing your ring." He nods to her bare left hand, and I swallow. I noticed the signs, but the outcome still feels like a blow.

Mom reaches across the table and squeezes his hand. "Don't be mad at your father. This is not just his fault." Ramsey nods, looking down at his plate to avoid her eyes.

We go back to eating after she squeezes my shoulder and I nod, still not sure what I want to say. Harley's hand stays on my knee, and I panic a bit, wondering if Mom can see. I shake my leg to try to warn him, but he leaves it there, eating quietly and seemingly unbothered.

"You want to go to the gym after this?" Ramsey asks Harley and he squeezes my knee once more as he nods, swallowing the food in his mouth.

"Sure."

We all eat some more in silence, and I push some eggs around as the boys get up and kiss Mom on the cheek before heading out. Harley looks back before they leave the room, catching my eye and giving me a half smile. I nod, reassuring him, but he frowns before leaving.

Once they are gone, Mom starts clearing the table and I get up to help.

"Everything prepped for dinner?" I ask, voice coming out more monotonous than I mean.

"Yes, everything's all set in the fridge for later, just needs to be put in the oven at the right times. Turkey's already defrosted."

I nod, following her into the kitchen with arms full of dishes.

"How are you doing, love?" Mom asks, setting down a half full tray of random things off the table. She takes the bowl of fruit off and walks over to the fridge.

I shrug, putting the bowl of scrambled eggs down and getting the cling wrap out.

"Be honest, Mira. I know you're not okay with this right now. I want to know what you're feeling." She takes the box from me after I cover the eggs and starts wrapping the tray of French toast.

I sigh. "I just don't understand what happened."

Mom abandons the tray and comes over and wraps her arm around my shoulders, putting the side of her head against mine. "I just realized I wasn't happy. Nothing happened, it just hit me one day. Dad hasn't been happy for a while either. He loves us, but he loves what he does too. And I think I pulled him away from that too much, not understanding he needed it."

I shake my head. "But why now?"

Mom sighs. "It started when Ramsey left for school. I had a little more free time since you were older and independent, so I started noticing how much time I spent distracting myself. Then you left for school, and I was alone here a lot." I wince and she rubs my back. "This is not your fault, Mira. It is not your job to look after me." She smiles, adding, "Yet," with a bump of her shoulder against mine. "We just realized we had grown apart well before we noticed it. I overcompensated for that loss by making my life about you and your brother and once you guys left the nest, I realized exactly how much I did that." She shrugs. She lifts her head, and I look her in the eye. "I know you're going to blame yourself but try not to. You always tried to take responsibility for my and your father's happiness ever since you were little and I tried so hard to curb that, but I could have done better." I start to shake my head, but she puts her hand on my cheek to stop me. "We can talk about this anytime you want, but I want to talk to you about school right now, before I forget."

"It's fine, Mom," I say, the fight in me gone, making the words sound hollow. She gives me a look, cocking her hip. I take a deep breath.

"I know you're not enjoying school, Mira." Her eyes push me over the edge.

"I hate my classes, Mom. I've been so stressed and ignoring it most of the time. The only class I like is my sketching course."

"I'm not surprised." She rubs my back a bit more, eyes pinched. "Art was always your favorite escape and you're so talented. If you want to switch to a BFA, I support you wholeheartedly." She smiles and I try to mimic it, Dad's postcards popping into my mind. "In fact, I insist on it. You should not be making life decisions based on my or your father's opinions, but since you already went with his choice and hate it, I insist you try this one since I know it's what you would pick for yourself."

I laugh, tears springing to my eyes. She wipes them away and nods. "Now that that's settled, what else is new in your life?" Her tone is leading, and I raise a brow, needing more to go off of. She clearly already knows something but wants me to tell her about it.

"Why are you asking like that?" I prompt when she just

smiles at me, before heading back to the table to finish clearing it. I follow, grabbing the pitcher of orange juice and carafe of coffee.

Mom shrugs, smiling still. "No reason. Just wondering how long you and Harley have been seeing each other?"

My heart stops and I nearly drop the juice, but I recover without spilling a drop. "We're not!" I insist, opening my mouth to deny it further.

"I saw him sneaking back to his room this morning, Amiria. So, unless he decided to sleep in the game room, I'm pretty sure I know what's going on."

I close my eyes, setting everything in my hands on the counter. "Maybe he was sleeping with Ramsey," I try.

Mom laughs and I glance over at her. "I thought that at first," she admits. "But given his attention to you at dinner last night and then breakfast this morning, not to mention your reaction right now, I think I can make a safe bet he spent the night with you." She walks over, rubbing my back again. "What's wrong?"

"We're not together, Mom." I sigh, tipping my head back and looking up at the ceiling. "We've just been sleeping together."

"Because you're scared of Ramsey's reaction?"

My head snaps back down, eyes meeting hers.

"No. Because Harley is. He thinks he'll lose Ramsey if he knows." Mom's brow furrows and I continue. "He thinks of us as his family now, after everything that happened with his parents." Mom nods. "He's scared if we cross that line, he'll lose all of us at once and can't handle being on his own after that."

Mom nods again, putting her hands on either side of my face. "I love you, but I have always considered Harley one of my kids. No matter what happens between the two of you, he will always be a part of this family." She smiles. "I will tell him that too. He's probably worried about his business loan as well, but I would never do anything to hurt him or the gym, even if things ended between you two."

I nod, feeling lighter.

She takes her hands away and smiles. "You two are naïve if you think Ramsey doesn't suspect by now either. Given his lack of accusation, I bet he won't have the reaction you guys have been picturing if you were to tell him."

My nose scrunches up as I follow her back to the table, stacking the plates and remaining dirty dishes so I can carry them back with her.

"Your brother loves you and he loves Harley. Even if he is mad at first, he'll realize that being against it will just hurt the both of you."

I shrug, staring down at the plates I'm carrying. I dump them in the sink.

Mom grabs my arm to stop me. "I think you two would be great together. You've both liked each other for so long and I'm happy you're both figuring it out."

"What do you mean?" I rub my temples, my brain not quite catching up to everything that's happened in the last forty-eight hours.

"I have eyes, Mira." She gives me a *don't be stupid* look. "You both have been crushing on each other even before they left for school."

I shake my head. "Harley didn't notice me back then. He thought of me as a kid sister before I kissed him at my fifteenth."

Mom smiles and rolls her eyes. "Harley never looked at you like a sister. He watched out for you and teased you, but he would watch you when you weren't paying attention the same way you would for him. I don't think either of you even knew you were doing it half the time." I frown and Mom nudges my shoulder again. "Boys don't do that if they see you as a sister," she adds before heading back to the table. I flip on the water, starting to wash the dishes, letting my brain work everything over.

22

Trees roll by at breakneck speeds as I stare out the window in the back of the Jeep once again. The last few days have been weird, not necessarily the stress-free break I could have used. After talking with Mom, I spent most of the day in my room, being pulled out by Harley and Ramsey who showed up hours later to get me out of the house. We went to the park and played basketball for a bit, the two of them obviously letting me win and picking me up a few times to help me dunk. I laughed every time, both of them smiling and threatening to drop me if I kept wiggling around. We got back just in time to help Mom set everything out for Thanksgiving dinner. Her parents called as usual halfway through the meal. Dad never showed up.

Harley laughs from the front seat, pulling my attention.

Ramsey left after dinner on Friday, going on a date and leaving Harley and me alone for a bit. We went for a walk in the woods, and he told me about the weirdest thing my mom said to him that morning. I laughed asking what she said, and he stopped me, pinning me against a tree and saying she told him she loved him and always would no matter what happens between him and me.

I laughed, wrapping my arms around his neck. "She saw you sneak back into your room yesterday morning." Harley swore, though a smile tinged his mouth. "She told me the same thing when she confronted me about it." Harley hummed, leaning forward to kiss down my neck. "Even said she thinks Ramsey wouldn't care," I added, biting my lip.

Harley pulled back, looking down at me with a wrinkled forehead. "Wouldn't care about what?"

My throat dried and I toyed with the hair at the back of his neck. I shifted on my feet; my stomach feeling weighed down with lead. "Us," I whispered, heart pounding.

Harley snorted, eyes searching mine. "Pretty sure he'd care about me fucking his sister, Mir." I flinched and he unconsciously rubbed my sides. I looked down and he sighed. "I don't want to fight," he whispered, kissing the top of my head and I nodded, pulling his head down to kiss him.

He fucked me against the tree, neither of us saying a word the whole time. When he took my hand and pulled me back toward the house, I hid the tears that slipped down my cheek.

Then I spent the rest of the weekend either with Mom or Ramsey around. Harley never snuck into my room again and we avoided each other whenever we accidentally ended up alone.

Harley looks back at me from the front seat when I stay quiet as Ramsey rambles. His brows furrow and I glance away, watching the trees. My phone buzzes and I pull it out, seeing Harley's name on my lock screen.

HARLEY

What's wrong?

I stare at the words, considering just ignoring him, but he glances over his shoulder, catching me looking at them. He follows up with another text.

HARLEY

You're quiet, Meerkat. What's on your mind?

I shake my head, trying to clear the fog settling.

Nothing. Just nervous about finals and getting back to classes.

Harley types quickly from the front seat.

HARLEY

Simple fix. Change your major. Then no more shitty classes.

I sigh, dropping my phone in my lap. Mom asked me if I was still thinking about switching before we left and I told her I was considering it, but I needed to focus to try not to absolutely tank my GPA in the next two weeks. She nodded, smoothed my hair, and told me not to stress too much, everything would work out.

Harley frowns at the windshield, and Ramsey eyes me in the rearview mirror again. I tune everything out, putting headphones in and turning my music up to full volume.

Bentley leans against the side of West Tower when we pull up, two to-go cups in his hands as he waits for me to get my bag from the trunk. Ramsey hugs me, pulling back but leaving his hands on my shoulders. "I love you, bug. Don't worry yourself too much, okay?" I nod and he swipes his fist lightly under my chin. "Cheer up. Once finals are over, we get to party. Harley's twenty-first is going to be a rager." He nods to his best friend, who has turned to watch us from the front seat. I chuckle, avoiding Harley's eyes and hugging Ramsey again. "Call me if you get sad," he whispers before releasing me and closing the trunk.

I walk over to Bentley who offers me a cup. "Extra fudgy hot chocolate. Figured you'd need it." I smile, watching my brother and Harley drive away before looking back at Bentley with tears in my eyes.

"Oh, Mir." He engulfs me in his arms, pulling me inside and out of the cold as I start to sob into his chest.

Things go weirdly back to normal for the last two weeks of school. It's like Harley forgets everything that happened at home, showing up to run and train every other day like we did before. The sex is a bit more disconnected, but he still spoons me afterward every time. It's like even though we both know this is running its course with my mom already in the know, we can't give up the physical connection we coveted throughout the semester, itching to touch each other.

I fumble my way through finals, only really smiling when I get to hand in my portfolio of sketch pieces for my art final. The sketches of Harley mysteriously went missing after he slept in my dorm but the folder has pieces of every other important person in my life.

My prof smiles, saying she's excited for this one. I breathe deeply for the first time when I step out of the building, the sharp drop in temperature the last few days making my face freeze instantly. I smile, nonetheless.

It's over. One semester down.

Bentley, Autumn, and Aria greet me when I meet them for lunch after, all of us cheering that it is finally over.

Janette hugs me before she leaves, catching me off guard as I brush my teeth. "I'm heading out," she says. She took her last final earlier that morning. We still have a few days before we have to be out of the dorm, but her mom bought her plane ticket back so they can spend as much of break together as they can.

I smile, spitting out toothpaste and hugging her back. "I'll see you in a few weeks," I say, and she nods. "Have a really good break."

"You too!" She smiles. "Text me if you need anything," she adds with a wink, and I chuckle and then the suite is empty.

I have one more training session with Harley before break. He plans to stay here for most of it since a lot of his trainers are students who head home on breaks. A good amount of the locals use the gym when all the students are away, and someone needs to be there to run things.

I skip into the nearly vacant gym, finding Harley already setting the mats up in the training room. I stretch and start my warmups, and he joins me halfway through. We've been slowly easing back into banter, but our silences still feel a bit tense.

I grin while I punch the padded mitts on his hands a little while later. "Your party's tonight." Harley grunts, whether a reaction or a response, I can't tell. I swing again. "Officially legal," I whistle.

He rolls his eyes. "Yeah, the last one of the group. I can finally stop worrying about my fake when I go out with them."

"I'm excited for the party tonight. Finals are over, I don't have to go to any classes tomorrow. I'm going to drink whenever Ramsey isn't looking." I chuckle, punching each of his mitts in a combo. "Plus, it's your birthday, so I'll have to come up with something special to give you before the end of the night." I waggle my eyebrows at him.

Harley stands up, dropping his hands. "We can't go sneaking off, you know that right? Ramsey will be watching us. I think he got a little suspicious over Thanksgiving."

I stand up, sweat rolling down my neck. I roll my eyes, gut clenching. "I know not to blow you in front of the party, Har."

Harley's face reddens and he rips off the mitts. "Quit acting childish. I'm serious." He turns and starts to walk away.

"I'm not acting childish." Anger whips through me and a fissure of resentment burns. "You're being a coward."

His head turns at that, eyes flashing with his own anger.

I step toward him. "You're too scared to tell Ramsey about us."

Harley crosses his arms. "You knew the deal when we made it." His voice is deadly low, and the tone makes me swallow harshly. "Why are you suddenly angry about the terms?"

"I'm not," I say, bite still evident. Harley quirks an eyebrow, eyes staring at me with condescension. "I've just don't think Ramsey will react as badly as you think he will. Even my mom doesn't think so."

His eyes narrow. "You're crazy if you think he'll just brush it off. He's way too protective of you not to think I've been trying to fuck you for years or that I've coerced you or something."

I step back. "Ramsey would never think that about you. You're best friends. He would never end your friendship over who you're in a relationship with."

Harley's spine snaps straight. "Relationship? Mira, we're just sleeping together. Have things started to feel deeper for you?"

I step back and force myself not to look away from him. My pulse pounds in my ears. "No," I say hastily, ice sluicing through my chest. "I just meant our situation. As friends with benefits."

Harley steps forward, leaning toward me a bit. "Then you said it yourself. Ramsey doesn't need to know about who you're just sleeping with. Especially since we're not even exclusive."

My chest explodes, the fissures that slowly formed in my heart breaking fully and pieces flying everywhere inside me.

He's been sleeping with other people.

I wondered about it a few times, but never got up the courage to ask. And now with him staring me dead in the eye and admitting it, I feel everything inside me shut down. The image of the girl straddling his lap on his bed from my birthday flashes in front of me and I wonder how many times he slept with her since he started sleeping with me. I turn away from him, going over to my phone and water bottle and grabbing them.

"Where are you going?" Harley's voice sounds resigned. When I look back at him, he's running his hand over his face.

"Forgot I told Bentley I'd meet him for coffee. Don't want to be late." I start toward the door, seeing his eyes flash at my best friend's name.

Harley's voice comes out deadly quiet, but the words hit my ears from across the room. "Well, it's probably better we don't fuck right now. You're not even the best I've had this week."

I stop dead in the threshold of the training room. Two

people work on machines in the main room. Cheryl sits behind the front desk as snow drifts down outside. I stare at the girl as she files her nails, remembering all the times she flirted with Harley, all the times he seemed to push her off. Was he just doing that because I was around? Was he fucking her in his office too?

My mind spirals, but I push it all down, drawing myself up and looking over my shoulder at him. He stands, eyes blazing, fists clenched at his sides in the same spot in the center of the mats.

"Go fuck yourself, Harley." I enunciate every syllable, seeing them hit as he clenches his teeth.

Rage shakes me as I vibrate out of the gym, grabbing my bag and jacket without bothering to put it on. Cheryl watches me storm out, eyes flitting back to the training room before the door closes behind me. I trudge down the road, walking the whole way back to campus without feeling the cold.

23

I storm all the way up to Bentley's room, banging on the door. Axel opens it, jumping out of the way when I don't even hesitate to knock him over as I enter.

"Whoa, Bentley, your girl is pissed," he yells.

Bentley appears, eyebrows touching. "What happened?"

I recount the scene at the gym, Bentley and Axel each pissed for me by the end. My anger subsides ever so slightly by the time I'm done. Seeing them irate helps.

"You want us to go beat the shit out of him?" Axel asks, standing to pace. I shake my head, smirking. Axel cracks his knuckles, whispering, "I can't believe he said that to you," under his breath.

Bentley catches my hand, pulling me down on the couch next to him. "What do you want to do?"

"I want to get drunk tonight." He nods. "I want to look hot and dance and drink and just let go of everything that's happened the last few weeks for a few hours before I have to deal with it all again."

Bentley hugs me and kisses the side of my head. "Okay,

Mir. I'll watch out for you tonight and DD. Go start getting ready." He pulls back with a smirk. "Wear red."

"Always."

I flounce back to my dorm. The boys start whispering before I even leave the room, but I don't catch any of what they say. I immediately start getting ready, knowing exactly the outfit I want to wear tonight.

I bought the dress for my eighteenth with Bentley when we took his parent's credit card to the city over the summer. He saw it in a window and made me try it on, the velvet material clinging and dipping everywhere it needed to. I throw on some sheer tights and red boots to match after spending some time on my makeup to accentuate my eyes and lips. Bentley shows up, dressed nicely, and hands me a leather jacket of his to wear on the walk. I smile, both of us knowing me in a man's jacket will stir up Harley. Especially if it's Bentley's. Axel offers his arm as we head downstairs and out of West Tower.

Bentley drives us over to the mansion, the party already well underway with cars littering the streets. We have to walk a little way down the road, and I huddle in Bentley's jacket, his arm slung around my shoulders as he tries to keep me warm with his body heat. Axel follows behind us with his hands in his pockets. The bass from the music inside thumps through me as we walk in, lights dim and people everywhere. I smile, grabbing a drink off the table next to the door and downing it. Bentley leaves his arm around me, surveying the room as we walk in. Autumn and Aria sit on one of the couches, Layla and Gwen talking to them. We start to head over, Axel taking Bentley's coat from my shoulders and going to find a place to store it, but Bentley and I are blocked on all sides as the Ravens converge.

Ramsey stands right in front of me, looking down at my dress. "Go home and change. It's twelve degrees out."

Bentley wraps his arm around me again. Harley stands behind the others, watching the movement with a tick in his jaw and fire in his eyes.

I smirk at my brother. "Good thing your house is heated." I try to walk around him, but his arm shoots out, blocking me.

"I'm serious, Amiria."

"I'm not a child, Ramsey," I warn, eyeing his arm before looking up to meet his eyes. "You don't get to try to dictate my choices like Mom and Dad did." I can feel the alcohol warming my insides and I hope it's the reason the words slide off my tongue.

Ramsey steps back, mouth open. "That's not what I was trying to do," he murmurs. Harley steps closer to him and my rage from earlier resurfaces.

"*Go home and change*," I mimic. "Sounds like a direct order to me."

Bentley squeezes my shoulder.

Ramsey rubs a hand down his face then looks at my best friend. He pokes Bentley in the chest as he speaks. "You. Watch her. I don't trust some of the guys here tonight." He glances down at me. "Have some fun, but please don't do anything too stupid."

I shake my head and brush past him, breaking out of Bentley's hold. I shoulder bump Harley as I pass, not looking back until I am a few steps away. He glares at me, the rest of the Ravens already dispersed, and then turns the glare on Bentley when he pushes past as well on the other side. I smirk, joining Autumn, Aria, Layla, and Gwen.

A few strong drinks later and I am past a nice buzz, right on my way to wasted. We meander through the house, finding the pool door locked when we try it, but explore the little office library on the other side of the kitchen when sitting on the couches gets boring. I sip my fifth or sixth drink, watching people dance in the open space of the main room.

"You should slow down," Axel shouts into my ear, and I shake him off, taking another gulp of my drink.

"I'm fine," I breathe, missing some of the letters when my tongue gets heavy. He nods, leaning against the table behind us, shoulder touching mine. Bentley brackets in my other side, the two rarely leaving me and never without the other being there.

"We should go play beer pong." I point to the tables set up in the big room on the other side of the stairs. Autumn claps, grabbing my arm and pulling me across the room toward one. Two guys stand at one end, a game just finishing. They look up when we approach, and I recognize the one who smiles as Derek from Harley's gym.

"Want to play?"

I nod, head bobbing a bit too much and we set up our side of the table. Autumn starts and we take turns, the guys beating us at first, but we take back the lead toward the end. When they have one cup left on their side and three on ours, I sink the winning ball and jump up and down. Autumn screams and Bentley laughs at the two of us.

Derek comes around the table, congratulating us.

"You want a rematch?" I ask. The room spins a bit, and I grab his arm to steady myself.

"I think getting beat by you once was enough." He chuckles. "How come I haven't seen you at these parties more often this year?" More people come in to play on the table we abandon, and we step back, leaning against a wall, facing each other. Bentley and Autumn go to find drinks,

Bentley tapping my shoulder and pointing out Axel who stands on the other side of the room watching me. I nod and roll my eyes at Axel who shakes his head and crosses his arms.

"Ramsey is my brother," I shout over the music. I have to lean in so Derek can hear, barely hearing myself over all the noise. "Kinda hard to party when he's breathing down your neck." My eyes stray at the mention of my brother, looking to see if he is watching me too, but finding a pair of grey eyes over the rim of a red solo cup, burning into my skull.

"Ah, so Ramsey has been hiding his hot little sister from all of us."

I giggle and turn back to stare into Derek's flat eyes.

He leans in closer, breath tickling the shell of my ear. "It'd be worth it to get punched by him and the boss for dancing with you."

I feel warm but am long past being able to discern if it's the alcohol or his words doing that. I look over his shoulder to where Harley has been glaring and find him grinning down at a brunette with curly hair. My blood boils and I hear his words from the gym earlier in my ears.

You're not even the best I've had this week.

I grab Derek's hand as he sloppily tries to kiss my neck and pull him back to the main room where people dance. I grab another drink off a table on the way, downing half before spinning around and facing Derek. His eyes are half-hooded, pupils blown, as he grabs my waist, and we start grinding against each other. I put my hands around his neck, pulling him closer to me and he returns his lips to my skin. I can feel him hard against my thigh as we sway and rock against each other. His hands slide down my waist and around, squeezing my ass. I close my eyes and sigh, picturing Harley biting into the crook of my neck where Derek lazily kisses.

Derek yanks away from me, the force of it almost toppling me on my heels. I open my eyes, finding Harley with his fist wrapped around Derek's collar, practically snarling in his face.

"Whoa, dude," Derek whines, hands up as his feet scramble, only his toes touching the ground. People scatter away from the scene, a ring forming around the three of us. "I didn't know you two were still a thing. I wouldn't have danced with her if I had."

"We aren't," Harley growls. I cross my arms over my chest. "She is Ramsey's little sister though." I roll my eyes. "And he would happily beat the shit out of you if he caught you basically fucking her in the middle of his living room." Except it's not Ramsey threatening Derek in the middle of the living room.

Harley's words make Derek pale though. His eyes scramble around the room and it must be liquid courage that makes him say, "She's an adult. She can make her own decisions. Ramsey's not even around right now." Harley's hand, that's not fisted in Derek's shirt, clenches. Derek's head rolls over to face me. "You want me to leave you alone, Mira?"

"Nooooo," I say, the room tipping again and my tongue slipping around in my mouth.

Harley's head whips over toward me. "How drunk are you?"

I try to stand up straighter, but the floor feels slippery. "None of your business." The words sound right in my head, but Harley's eyes search my face faster.

He turns back to Derek. "Leave." He drops him, turning

toward me. Derek falls forward, catching himself, but my eyes lock with Harley's.

"I'm taking you home." He pulls me by the arm, making me stumble behind him a few feet as the room spins.

My stomach rolls and I have enough time to mutter, "Uh oh," before puking all over the floor and Harley's shoes.

I hear people groan and shout. Harley yells, "Party's over, everyone out!" as the music cuts out and the lights get turned on. I hunch over, hands on my knees, breathing slowly and trying to stop the convulsions starting in my abdomen.

"Come on," Harley murmurs, gripping my shoulders and pushing me through people over to a bathroom. He leans over the toilet as I puke again, lightly taking the scrunchie off my wrist, gathering my hair and cinching it. Then he starts rubbing my back. He makes soothing noises while tears prick my eyes and stream down to my chin.

I hear Bentley at the door as he says, "Fuck, Mira." I wave over my shoulder as my stomach clenches and my body shakes. "I left for two seconds and then couldn't find you again."

"I watched her the whole time," Axel says.

I feel Harley's grip on my hair tighten. "And you let that guy grope her?" His voice bites out.

"She pulled him onto the dance floor." Axel's voice rises. "She's allowed to have fun."

I puke again.

"Yeah, she's having a ton of fun now," Harley mumbles as he rubs my back again.

"I'll take her home," Bentley says, sounding closer this time.

I flush the toilet, still leaning over and closing my eyes.

"She won't make it through a bumpy car ride, not even

for five minutes, and she can't walk that far in the cold." Harley says. "She can stay here tonight. I'll put her in my room. I can make sure she's okay."

I whimper, wanting to respond but scared if I open my mouth, I'll puke again.

"You are not looking after her," Bentley starts, but Harley cuts him off.

"I would never let anything happen to her," he barks. I squeeze my eyes closed and shiver.

"I'm more worried about *you* happening to her," Bentley hisses. I open my eyes, looking over my shoulder to see them chest to chest, anger radiating through the room. Axel stands in the doorway, chest puffed, and arms crossed.

Fear lances through me, and I don't take the time to figure out who exactly it's for as I stand up. The room spins and I must sway because Harley reaches out and steadies me.

"He's right, Bent, I'm not making it back tonight. I'll find Ramsey. Don't worry."

"Are you sure, Mira?" Axel asks. My eyes flick over to him, and I nod before groaning when the movement starts a pounding in my head.

Bentley steps around Harley, kissing the top of my head. "Okay, Mir. I'll be come get you when you text in the morning." I reach out and grip his hand before he glares at Harley one more time and then leaves with Axel. The house is quieter, but I can still hear some people in the main rooms.

"Are you going to puke again?" Harley asks, reaching out to move some hair off my temple and rub the side of my head.

I twist away from him, his face pinching for a moment.

"Or do you want to go lie down?" he asks, smoothing his face out and trying to hide his reaction with a head tilt.

I walk over to the sink, turning on the faucet and cupping the water before sipping it from my palm. I swirl it around my mouth before spitting it back out. Glancing at myself in the mirror, I groan at how disheveled I look, eyes bloodshot and lipstick basically gone.

I walk slowly out of the bathroom, ignoring Harley calling my name as he follows. Nobody really remains, the last few people already putting coats on by the door. I flop down on the couch, Smith laid out on the carpet beside it, passed out with cups all over him. My stomach settles as I rub it and close my eyes. A blanket covers me, and I find Harley covering me, tucking the end under my feet the way I like.

"What happened?"

I glance over the stairs as Ramsey flies down them to where I lay.

"She drank too much," Harley says, stepping back and crossing his arms. "Puked in the living room so I called it and sent everyone out. She's still sick so I figured she could stay the night."

Ramsey leans over the back of the couch, smoothing my hair down. "You want some water?" I nod and he disappears, coming back a moment later with a clear glass. I sit up and sip it slowly, feeling Harley stare at me.

"You should sleep in a bed, bug. Take mine. I can take you upstairs."

I wave him off. "The couch is fine, I swear." Ramsey starts to argue, but I snuggle down into the blanket. "It's super comfy, I swear."

Ramsey sighs, leaning down to kiss my forehead. "Okay, Mir. Text me if you need anything. I'm going to go crash." He stands back up and walks upstairs, calling out goodnight to me and Smith.

I close my eyes and settle down, tucking my hands underneath my cheek and settling down on a throw pillow. My head swims and I try to find a rhythm to the waves as I start to doze off.

Hands lift me up, cradling me against a solid chest and my eyes fly open. Harley carries me over to the stairs, starting to ascend them.

"What are you doing?" I ask, squirming in his arms.

He speaks evenly as he walks up the stairs, not looking down at me. "You're sick. You need to sleep in a bed not a couch." He walks down the hall and into his room, placing me down on his bed. I scramble to sit up, but his hand presses into the center of my chest, forcing me gently to lay down.

"You're insane if you think I'm going to sleep next to you on your bed," I spit.

Harley covers me with his comforter, tucking my feet in again.

"I'm taking the couch, Mira." He smooths down my hair. "No one has slept here besides me," he adds, looking me in the eye.

I roll my eyes. "I know that's a lie." I start to sit up again.

Harley pushes me down once more. "The furthest I've gone in this room is a shitty make out one time, Mir. Just go to sleep. You'll feel better sleeping here and I won't touch you, I promise."

I bite the inside of my cheek as he walks away and turns out the light, glancing back over at me with a weird look in his eyes.

"What?" I bite out as he hesitates.

"I haven't—" he cuts himself off, seeming to come back

to the present from wherever he got stuck in his head. "Nothing," he says, shaking his head. "Go to sleep. There's Advil in the bathroom medicine cabinet if you need it." He closes the door behind him, leaving the smallest crack so that I'm not left completely in the dark. I stare at the light beam, wondering what Harley had been about to say before he held himself back.

I pass out, picturing his eyes as he held Derek up and the feeling of his hand rubbing my back soothingly.

24

Mira

Someone swipes hair off my sweaty forehead, and I groan as the world comes back into sharp focus. My mouth feels like I ate sand and my eyelids slam shut immediately when I try to open them.

"Easy, Mir," Ramsey soothes.

I try to open my eyes again, sunlight filling the room now and making them sting to look around.

Ramsey gets up and lowers Harley's blinds. "Better?"

I nod, groaning again when the freight train running over my temples starts to protest.

"I brought juice and Advil." He comes back to sit on the side of the bed as I start to sit up. He points to the bedside table, and I reach out and take the pills and glass of cranberry juice, downing them one after the other.

"You're lucky you have two older brothers." He chuckles.

"What do you mean?" I croak and the words scratch their way out. I clear my throat.

"Me and Harley." He leans back on one hand. "I was too drunk to be of any help when everything happened last night so you're lucky you have Harley too."

"Harley is not my brother," I insist, twisting his comforter in my hands.

Ramsey chuckles and I look up at him. "I see your crush is still alive and well."

My brow furrows. "I don't have a crush."

"Mira, come on." He reaches forward and pats my hand. "I know you've always liked Harley as more than a friend. You idolized him when we were kids. It was obvious."

I roll my eyes, pulling my hand away. "I got over that, Ramsey. I'm not a kid anymore."

Ramsey smirks at me. "Sure," he says with a slight shoulder roll.

"I got over it," I insist. "I had to. I would never do anything to get in between you two." My stomach twists when I think about all the things I've done that would do just that.

It's over though. It has to be over now.

Ramsey chuckles and leans back toward me. "Thank you for considering me, Mir, but you don't need to." My eyes widen and he takes my hand in both of his. "About what you said last night, I'm sorry if I've made you feel like I was trying to dictate what you could do in any way. I just wanted to watch out for you."

I grip his hand, starting to stop him.

"No, listen. I never want you to ever feel like you need to make decisions about your life to please other people. It's what you've always done with Mom and Dad, and I didn't realize I might be on that list too." He pauses, letting the words sink in. "I know you're not a kid anymore. You can make your own decisions, and I want you to do whatever makes *you* happy. I will always support and look out for you, Mir."

I smile. "Thank you." My voice wobbles a bit as my throat dries.

Ramsey squeezes my hands. "And obviously you can date whoever you want." He drops my hand. "If that's Harley, then I'll support it. But I should warn you. Harley is my best friend, and I love him, but he's always been flakey with girls. He never really takes relationships seriously and they never last long. If you want to go for it, I'm not stopping you, but just," he sighs, running a hand through his curls. "Just use caution there, bug." He leans forward and gives me a quick hug. I stop breathing, brain blank throughout Ramsey's whole speech. "And know I won't take sides in any fights," Ramsey adds as he pulls back with a smile.

I chuckle, a smile spreading on my face until Harley's words float back into my short-circuited mind.

You're not even the best I've had this week.

My smile falls as my stomach sinks. I shake my head. "It was just a dumb crush." I look down at the comforter, twisting the maroon fabric between my fingers. "Nothing's going to happen."

Ramsey watches me for a moment before shrugging. "Okay, if that's what you want." He stands up and glances at his watch. "I have to go to an interview for a new TA spot. Fingers crossed I get it, so I don't have to keep working under Jenkins."

I hear the floor in the hallway creak, one of the guys probably waking up just as hungover as me.

"If I get it, I'll be so much less stressed next semester before graduation."

I nod and he picks up the empty glass from the bedside table.

"Stay as long as you want. I don't know how long I'll be

gone, but just lock up behind you if no one is here when you leave."

I nod and he smiles.

"I'll pick you up tomorrow morning." He leans down and pecks the top of my head before walking out.

I sit on Harley's bed for a few minutes looking around. This is my first time inside this room. It's fairly tidy with a few shirts on the floor beside the laundry bin, but otherwise not much out of place. He has a desk with some papers meticulously organized in a few places around an open laptop. Some framed photos sit next to a bottle of air freshener, and I chuckle. I'm sure my mom gave him all that since I can't really picture Harley at the store picking out frames. I get up and walk over, noting the freshener's cranberry scent. Definitely from my mom.

Leaning down to look at the photos, I smile and accidentally bump the laptop. Harley's screen lights up and my smile instantly falls when I see his lock screen.

It's a collage of pictures, the Ravens, him and Ramsey in their old football gear, random scenery from hikes and around town.

My eyes freeze on picture of me though. Just me, laughing at the camera. Ramsey took it after Bentley teamed up with him and told me some dumb joke, making me snort when I laughed. It was taken last summer.

Before I left for school and started anything with Harley.

I touch it, wondering how he even got it, why he made it part of his lock screen, *when* he made this his lock screen. My mind spirals, the culmination of this semester crashing down on me over and over again as I stare at myself in that photo.

The screen goes black, and I step back. So many

emotions swirl through me, and I can't seem to pick them apart. Confusion about where we stand. Anger and hurt over what he said yesterday. A dull ache at Ramsey's confession that the two of us together wouldn't bother him.

The most dominant feeling though is that I just want to go home.

I close my eyes and consider texting Bentley. He'll want to pick me up, but the walk will be a good way to start getting over the hangover.

I sigh. I need coffee.

I leave the room, wandering down the stairs and toward the kitchen. Smith no longer lays on the carpet, and I breeze past the island, stepping over discarded cups and debris. Someone must have cleaned up my puke because the floor is clear of it. I plug the boys' coffee machine in, searching the cabinets for grounds.

"Morning."

I jump and spin around. Harley stands at the previously vacant island, face drawn. I close my eyes and breathe to calm my racing heart. As the scare wears off, anger starts to set in. The image of my photo in his lockscreen collage and my brother's words clash with everything Harley has said to me about the two of us all semester.

You're not even the best I've had this week.

My hands shake as I turn back to the coffee maker, filling the pot with water and pouring it into the back of the machine.

"I heard you talking with Ramsey."

I pause and stare out the back window over the sink. Snow lays on the ground, but the day is sunny and bright, shining off the top of it.

"Which part?" I ask.

Harley drags back a stool, sitting down. "The whole thing."

I close my eyes before returning to the task at hand. So, he knows. He knows Ramsey wouldn't give a damn if we were together. And hasn't this whole time.

The machine starts to percolate, and I cross my arms, staring down at it, willing it to go faster so I can escape. "I'll be gone after I have some coffee."

"Mira. You can stay however long you want."

I shake my head, still not facing him.

The coffee starts to drip out into the pot, and I go searching for a mug, setting it next to the machine and then getting the milk and sugar.

"Mira," Harley tries.

I pour milk into my mug, filling it about halfway then adding the sugar and stirring it together.

"Mira," he pleads.

"I think we should stop training together." My voice comes out clear, but I have to swallow after speaking.

His chair scrapes back quickly, and I hear him hastily get up.

"I'm going home for the break, and I don't think I'm going to have time for it with my schedule next semester." I shrug and the words hang in the air as the coffee keeps pouring out.

"We can make it work," he finally says, voice determined. "I'll rearrange my schedule. Drop a client if I have to."

Tension invades my stomach. I turn to face him. His eyes rove my face, lips turning up fractionally even as his shoulders bunch, and his hands grip the edge of the island.

I shake my head. "I don't want to take up any more of your time."

His face falls. "What? You're not 'taking up my time.'" He sighs, looking around and running his hands through his hair for a moment. "I look forward to spending time with you, Meerkat."

The nickname bounces off me, usually lifting my spirits when he uses it.

"I like training you." He looks down at the island, running his hand over the edge. "I like *you*."

I wait for the giddy reaction, sealing myself off from it. But nothing comes. Nothing but a gnawing at my ribs. This is all too fucking late.

"And Ramsey said he'd be okay with us. Maybe, when you guys get back from break, we can sit down with him, and—"

"No." I lean back against the counter, the warmth from the coffee machine seeping through my dress and waking me up a bit more.

Harley just watches me, eyes tense.

"No, Harley. I can't do this anymore." I cross my arms. "Ramsey may be fine with the idea of us, but he was right. You're not serious about this. You've made it clear being with me openly isn't something you want." He starts to speak, and I hold my hand up. "You might say it is right now or for the next few days, but this whole semester, you've been hot one minute and cold the next." Panic seeps into his expression. "I'm tired of feeling like your dirty little secret." I take a deep breath, pushing past the spiky pain in my chest. "I want to end this."

"Mira, no. I *am* serious about this. I—"

"*You're not even the best I've had this week,*" I reiterate, the words feeling as if they've seeped into the morrow of my bones.

Harley draws up short, body jolting before he freezes, mouth left open and eyes wide.

"That's what *you* said, Harley." I step toward him, the island still separating us. "To hurt me. And it worked." My voice squeaks and the back of my throat instantly dries. I shake my head. "I don't blame you for sleeping with other people. We never said we were exclusive."

His brow crinkles, lips turned down. "Mira, no. I haven't —" He sighs, looking away and dragging his hand through his hair again. "When I said that, I was upset. You were talking about telling Ramsey and then you mentioned Bentley, and I—

"No!" I slam my palms down on the island, the stinging pain centering my anger. Harley's breath stutters, hands falling limply back to his sides. "You don't get to say that and then brush it off and blame me!" My cheeks heat and the back of my throat dries. "You *hurt* me, Harley. And I knew you were going to!" I laugh mirthlessly, hands shaking. My chin wobbles as the anger starts to give way. "I went into this knowing that it would end badly for me. But I thought I knew what kind of hurt I was signing up for when we started." I breathe in shakily. Everything churns inside me, excruciatingly hot under my skin. "You're not the guy I thought you were."

Something in him seems to wilt, and for a moment, sick satisfaction crawls up my throat. But it just gives way to more pain. Even now, I still don't like hurting him.

I sigh. "We're done, Harley." I turn back to the coffee maker, pulling the now full pot out and pouring it over my premade milk and sugar mixture.

Harley stays frozen behind me, not making a sound. I wait for his next move, listening to the ringing of the spoon against the mug as his presence behind me looms. Finally, the sound of his retreating footsteps slowly fades away. I listen to him walk upstairs, his bedroom door banging closed.

My stomach turns and after a few forced sips of coffee, I pour the rest down the sink.

Time to go home and get back to the way things were before.

25

Harley

uck.

Fuck. Fuck. *Fuck.*

I pace my room, stomach twisting and sweat forming across the back of my neck.

I fucked up. I knew it the moment I opened my stupid mouth and let my jealousy spill out yesterday at the gym. I just needed Mira to get the idea of telling Ramsey out of her head.

Gripping the hair at the sides of my head, I heave breaths in and out as I spiral over losing the only girl I think I've ever loved.

The last few minutes replay in my mind. The pain in her eyes. How resigned she sounded. Her back as she turned away.

We're done, Harley.

My eyes slowly close, hands pulling to the point of pain. Something sharp slides around inside me.

I can't blame her for any of it. Her pain is fully on me, but...we can't just be done.

I slam my fist down on my desk and light hits my closed eyelids.

Why the fuck did I lie to her?

You're not the guy I thought you were.

I open my eyes to find my laptop lock screen on. Mira's smiling face blares back at me.

Shit.

I'm not.

Dread floods my entire system, stomach plummeting and arms falling loosely to my sides.

I'm not the guy she thought I was. The guy who deserves to be with her.

But I can be.

I pull out my desk chair and sit down, determination simmering in my gut. Logging into my laptop, a mantra beats through the back of my mind.

I'm going to fix this.

THANK YOU FOR READING

Harley and Mira's story is the beating heart of the Imperium Coast series and I am so thankful you took a chance on the start to their story. If you liked it, please leave a review! Even just a star ranking really helps out indie authors like me. Your support means everything to me!

Harley and Mira will get their second chance.

In the meantime, check out TRUE BLUE, Janette, Bentley, and Axel's story, with an overlapping timeline to this book.

Curious about what's going on with Autumn and Ramsey?

Check out their story, GREEN LIGHT, up next! Green Light is an enemies to lovers, he falls first and harder, best friend's brother romance! (And there may be some Mira and Harley sightings along the way...)

ACKNOWLEDGMENTS

Thank you firstly, to you, the reader for spending some time in the Imperium Coast world. Seeing Red was the first book I wrote, not only for this series, but in the contemporary romance genre. The last three years since I wrote the first draft have been spent questioning each subsequent draft (and myself as a writer several times). The only reason you were able to read this final version is because of the abundance of amazing support I fortunately had along the way:

Kayla: my OG alpha reader, thank you for hyping me up as I maniacally outlined seven books and then word vomitted each of them to you to make sure my 2am fever dream wasn't completely crazy. Thank you for reading that very early Seeing Red draft all those years ago. You helped me believe I could actually publish them and I am forever grateful. And thank you for your continued support since then.

Kristen and Rachel: thank you for reading that early draft as well and letting me talk about all the random indie author things I sometimes need to vent to the nearest. You both helped push me to figure out how to make this book a reality.

Grace, Cat, Mitch, and Alex: thank you so much for constantly hyping me up, especially when I'm bad at doing it myself. You all have been massively supportive of my writing (which I shouldn't be surprised by at this point but sometimes I just can't help it) and I am so thankful to have you all in my corner.

Nikki: thank you thank you thank you for not only your art, but your line edits and constant availability for my random questions and thoughts. You've helped so much over the last few years and I am so thankful I can randomly text you at three in the morning to ask for a commission or a random birthday cake!

Sam: thank you so much for your beta comments! You helped me shape the middle version of this story and were the first person I asked to read it who didn't necessarily *have* to say it was good. I am so grateful that you took the time and so glad we got the opportunity to meet this summer!

Kristin: sorry again for the ending, I promise I will make it up to you eventually (may take you up on that Misery scenario just to get them done). Thank you so much for your support and time. You're literally one of the best (and most genuine) hype women I've ever met and I always walk away from a conversation with you feeling like I actually am a good writer and not just three raccoons in a trench coat banging on a keyboard 🖤

Spencer: thank you so much for not looking at me weird when I told you I was publishing a book. I am forever grateful for your support in literally everything and I could not ask for a better brother. Maybe one who texts back instead of calling but otherwise no notes.

Sheeda, Francesca, Courtney, Madison, and Jordan: thank you so much for that week we spent in the woods. WWTS gave me access to a whole community, but I will be eternally thankful that the six of us ended up in the same place at the same time (twice?!?!) because of it. Thank you all for helping me struggle through edits on this one, and maybe one day I will be confident enough to put *novellone* in Seeing Red's title. ¡Viva la *novellone*!

Thank you again to everyone who took the time to read my words. The process for Seeing Red was long and fraught with doubt, but I am so glad this book made it through and I really hope you enjoyed it!

ABOUT THE AUTHOR

Alacia (pronounced uh-lace-ee-uh) Hale is a contemporary romance writer with a penchant for messy and angst-ridden chaos characters. She loves writing stories filled with devotion, banter, and spice, a mixture that often leads down some intense and twisty paths. When she is not writing, you can find her drawing, travelling, or trying to keep another doomed plant alive. She currently lives in Upstate NY with her best friend, grumpy black cat, crazy orange kitten, and a head full of fictional people.

Want to keep up with everything Lacy and her future releases? Sign up for her newsletter to get regular updates.

ALSO BY ALACIA HALE

<u>The Imperium Coast Series</u>

True Blue: A Why Choose University Romance

Seeing Red: A First Chance University Romance

Green Light: An Academic Bully Romance

Yellow Card: A College Hockey Romance

White Knuckled

Grey Area

Red Duet Part II

9 781966 629802 1